GAME OF CHANCE

By
Jo Anne Algiers &
Richard Ansell

PublishAmerica
Baltimore

© 2006 by Jo Anne Algiers & Richard Ansell.
All rights reserved. No part of this book may be reproduced, stored in a retrieval system or transmitted in any form or by any means without the prior written permission of the publishers, except by a reviewer who may quote brief passages in a review to be printed in a newspaper, magazine or journal.

First printing

At the specific preference of the author, PublishAmerica allowed this work to remain exactly as the author intended, verbatim, without editorial input.

ISBN: 1-4241-2507-3
PUBLISHED BY PUBLISHAMERICA, LLLP
www.publishamerica.com
Baltimore

Printed in the United States of America

Dedications:

This is for my newly born grandchild, Owen Patrick Ansell, a new star in my heaven, and for Jo, without whom my "Chance" would never have been taken...R.A.

For my mother, who has been beside me every step in every way and for Richard, who saw it through to the final day—J.A.

We must acknowledge the spirit of Lizzie Borden and her help with our story...

"Lizzie's Legend"
Lizzie Borden took an axe
And gave her mother forty whacks
When she saw what she had done
She gave her father forty one...

During the morning of Thursday August 4th 1892, at the Borden family home at 92 Second Street, Fall River, Massachusetts; the dead bodies of Andrew J. Borden and his second wife Abby, were discovered, both had been murdered with a heavy sharp object, supposedly an axe, although the number of blows was not quite as extensive as the rhyme suggests.

Lizzie Borden lived at the family home with her Father, her stepmother, her sister and an Irish servant girl; Mr. Borden although quite a rich man, was renowned for his meanness, and it is a known fact that Lizzie did not get on with her stepmother, addressing her as Mrs. Borden, rather than Mother.

There was certainly strong suspicion, if not actual evidence of cruelty towards Lizzie, emotional if not physical and possibly actual abuse and it is believed that maybe she finally snapped and killed them both, however...

After collating much evidence, and changing suspects several times, the Police finally charged Lizzie, and she was brought to trial some ten months after the murders, and during the trial much was made of the horrible gory details of the crime, and many newspapers even then, just like nowadays, speculated as to her guilt without redress to much actual fact.

Finally, after a lengthy trial, Lizzie was found not guilty by the jury and acquitted of the terrible crime of parricide...

Like many crimes especially those remaining unsolved, these murders have grown into a legend, with much speculation and writing over the ensuing years; the house at number 92, has been turned into a bed and breakfast establishment, and still to this day, you can choose to spend the night in the very bedroom in which one of the murders was committed.

We offer no opinion or solution to this case, although many have tried over the years, but merely a few salient facts so that the readers of our story will understand to whom and what we refer to when we mention "Lizzie."

As for our story, no semblance to anyone, living or dead is meant, for the benefit of our tale, the names have been changed, to protect the guilty.

~Zach~

I never really knew what I wanted to do when I grew up, and so some would say it took me a long time to do so. Many say I haven't grown up yet—hell, I'm still a kid at heart

College was never a problem; I had the kind of mind that soaked up facts like a sponge. For a long time I just never knew what to do with it, or if any of it was worth storing, of course it always is, but at 18 you don't realise it will come in handy somewhere along the way.

For a while I thought I wanted to be a serious actor. Zachary Austin Murdock, the new Olivier, a young Brannaugh, and so found myself in London at stage school, RADA to please my mother and her family, trying to become something I never was, too analytical I guess, and just drifting really; at the same time, I had this fanciful dream of becoming a gentleman gambler, like the old riverboat card players, sort of Maverick without the hat; or with it—I knew I had the rakish air to carry it off, but even that wasn't realistic, mainly because I wasn't that good at it, as was told to me by someone who *was* very good. Who, in a very short time, became not only my greatest friend, but, the guy who would push me in the direction I was meant to go, and simply by an almost throwaway remark, one evening after I had lost yet again at cards, he said to me...' why don't you use that analytical mind for something it would be good at, and join the police force?'

Knowing Chance, which I came to do very well, I think it was almost a joke, a tongue in cheek remark, made to mostly tell me I was not good enough to live in his world, well, not professionally anyway; and so when I took his advice, and joined the L.A. Police Academy, he was quite surprised, but in a strange way quite proud, that he had made the suggestion that saw me finally find where I belonged.

So here I am, a Lieutenant of Detectives, progressing nicely, and enjoying, or at least finding satisfaction in what it is that I do now, and if I say so myself, do rather well, you could say I'm lucky, I've found where I belong, and I'm comfortable, and in no longer striving to please my parents, I think I somehow have.

Once in a while though, the need to step outside the comfort zone overcomes me, and I feel the need to live dangerously, not in the physical sense, that happens enough with the job, but mentally, to see once more whether I can play with the big boys in the card world; I'm reasonably well off, the job pays okay, but my family, makes up the LAPD shortfall in cash—I am, after all a member of a minor aristocratic line on mum's side, and must be compensated for that, so I am well provided for as such, and they are finally happy with me having a direction in my life, so when I sometimes dabbled with the old life, nobody disapproves too much, at least that I know of.

Chance and I would meet up, here or in London, or sometimes somewhere different. It was, for both of us, ostensibly to relax and enjoy a holiday, but in reality, to play cards. I never made much money at it, although I had my moments, but I always enjoyed trying. Of course I enjoyed the company of my friend, and though we didn't see each other that often, we had that kind of relationship, where it didn't matter, when we were together, it simply became like we always were, and even if I didn't play well, watching him play was always a pleasure.

I have had girlfriends, but never anything that became serious. I guess that was the only thing missing now, someone to be with, to be close to, and to share my life with; yes that was what I wanted now, something that would last for life, however long that was.

I guess things happen when they're meant to, and in whatever way fate decides, I hadn't expected to meet someone through a case, but that's the way it panned out, and though the case was baffling, one thing was clear. I had met someone who was to become very important to my life, someone who would change my luck, better my hand so to speak, and I couldn't wait to introduce her to my friend, the first time I had ever felt the need to do so; so I asked him to fly over and meet her, and chat over the case with me, he always brought his own brand of quirky analysis to things, and of course I wanted his opinion of my girl and how I felt and I couldn't wait for Chance to meet her. Elizabeth, my Ellie...

~Chance~

London was its usual perfumed-lady self, a mixture of decaying refuse and hot-dog onions, neon lights fizzing, and reflecting on rain slicked concrete. If you squinted, it had the look of a Monet painting. If you kept your eyes wide open, as well as your nose, it hit you like a well swung punch.

I'd left the flat in Queensway, where I lived among neighbours I didn't know, mostly Arabs, who could pretend they were still devout Muslims whilst they indulged in gambling, alcohol and women, but blame it on London, rather than their own desires; and rich girls, living off Daddy's old money and thinking they were independent as they shoved their monthly allowance up their noses with aplomb, and a disdain for the class and history of their own families.

I threaded the Jag in and out of the night-time traffic, dodging taxis who thought they owned the road, and did, and the saloon cars of people who came here once a month for a theatre trip and an overpriced meal just so that they could say they lived the London lifestyle.

I was heading for Kilburn tonight, not exactly the most salubrious part of town, and if you weren't West Indian or Irish, you were in the minority. But at least there, you lived among real people, not Home Counties yuppies who really were country people pretending to be Londoners.

I'd had a sort of word of mouth invitation to a game at an upstairs room of the Crown, a long time Irish pub, which at one stage in the sixties and early seventies, you wouldn't be caught dead in, unless you were either Irish or at least had sympathy with 'the boys', because you'd have a tin shaken under your nose, and be expected to contribute to the cause of the IRA, and if you didn't, you would become suddenly very unpopular, and in great danger of needing a long stay in hospital, or an even longer one in the cemetery.

These days, with the almost cessation of hostilities, and everyone talking up the new age and 'the peace process', you were as safe here as anywhere in any big city, which is to say not safe at all, unless you belonged, and I always had, nationalities didn't matter to me, I was London born and bred, this was my town.

The Paddy's had managed to save up for another lesson, and I was off to a five grand sit down, eight players; so we'd all sit down with our chips, and whoever was last man standing would walk out with Forty Thousand pounds, sterling, not bloody Euros, so help me I'd never play for Euros, might as well play for Monopoly money.

I parked the Jag outside a private house about a hundred yards from The Crown, and palmed a fiver to a grinning 10 year old… "if it's unscathed when I come out, I'll give you another, if there's one scratch on it, I'll hunt you down and eat your liver."
He slipped the five pounds into his pocket and grinned, 'make it another tenner and we'll wash it for you'; I laughed and said okay, well, we all got to make a living don't we?

As I stood at the bar and ordered a large Hine, well, it was 9pm, I used my mobile to check my home phone for messages, just in case, and there was something, something that lifted my spirit's a bit, took me out of the mundane, and made me smile.

The voice was Doc's—Zach Murdoch, my best friend, apart from the queen of diamonds; (I'd once drawn the queen to make a royal flush in diamonds, and won several thousand pounds, which then had been a lifeline…) he wanted me to come over to L.A. and discuss a case with him, one that was puzzling even his analytical mind, but really, even though he threw it in last of all, as a nothing; I knew the real reason, he'd met a woman, well a girl anyway, and he wanted me to meet her, wanted my 'approval'. Oh well, everything has to end, and it sounded from his voice as if our bachelor days might be drawing to a close, or at least his, the way he spoke about her, although only briefly, I knew, he was in deep; and so I had to go over and meet her. If only I'd known in advance just what that would mean, I'd have thrown the mobile into the bin and gotten drunk instead; but then hindsight always makes things easier don't it, otherwise nothing would be left to chance.

So when I wandered out into the morning air six hours later and with thirty five grand of Paddy's hard earned in my pocket, I was smiling, and thinking of breakfast, sleep, and a first class ticket to L.A. and seeing my friend again, and the simple enjoyment of living, and after all, what else was I going to do with all this lovely money, what's that old saying? 'Money won is always sweeter than money earned' well in my case it was both, won and earned, this was what I did, this was how I lived.

The kid was still there, sitting on an old dining chair, watching my car and two others, I wasn't sure if the two Micks would pay him, after the pasting they'd taken from me, so I bunged him twenty, and he waved to me as I drove away; if only I'd known, I would have given him the whole lot, set him up for life, and gone to live a quiet life by the seaside, but that's life ain't it, we never see it coming until it hits us, and by then it's too late, we've bought the ticket, and when I buy the ticket, even if the hostess is ugly, I still have to dance, can't resist the game, that's why I'm called Chance, well that and it's me name.

~Elizabeth~

I guess I was an accident waiting to happen, a haphazard window of opportunity looking for that toss of the dice that would finally pay off. Always looking to please and locking myself away in trying so hard to accommodate, to please, saving up all the chances to reciprocate until they all were tumbling down and almost buried me.

I was slowly deteriorating for the first 12 years of my life; I accepted what was presented to me. Then there is the coincidence of me finding The Diary, but, does it really exist, coincidence? Or is it just us having a need to explain what we really make happen by our own hand.

Why did I of all people find The Diary? Maybe that is what destiny is. I had always liked flea markets, but why on that fateful, overcast Saturday, did I pick up that leather bound volume, and when I did, why did it immediately feel like I had to have it, almost as if it were mine, and simply being returned to where it had always belonged; and the two dollars I paid for it seems like a small price doesn't it, for something that changes your life, or in fact defines it, gives it shape, makes it become what I suppose it was always meant to.

But then why did the other things have to happen, why did Zach have to come along? Oh yes, perhaps it was to show me there was a way out, through love, through appreciation. But of course by then it was too late wasn't it? In the end, what made my knight in shining armor a knight, would take him away from me; what I needed was a knight in tarnished armor…

CHAPTER ONE
~Elizabeth Ann Morse~

Chance labeled me a non-entity. I prefer it this way; I come and go as I please, unnoticed. At first…Unknown I am no one's friend and no one's acquaintance. I AM because I AM NOT. Confused? Good, that's how I wish the world in general to remain. —I am an evanescent entity.

I have not always been an unacknowledged presence. There was a time when I craved the limelight, mainly because the parents craved it for me. They chose to live their worthless lives through me. Pushing me before camera, shoving words down my throat, enjoying the praise they had never received personally through my accomplishments. Elizabeth Ann Morse, the apple of everyone's eye at the age of two, three, four and five. I learned to laugh, cry and flinch on cue. The flinching came quite naturally as I had been doing it as long as I could recall. One learns quickly the art of self preservation.

I was touted as being a "quick study"—a one take wonder. A couple of commercials for toothpaste, cartoon character shaped vitamins and a nasty tasting sugar free children's breakfast cereal that I was able to eat heartily and with a smile, led to several television spots and films with talk of a T.V. show centered around my amazing aqua eyes and skin the color of warm café' au' lait. The parents were in seventh heaven and living the life they had longed to grow accustomed to. Unfortunately part of the lifestyle for the father included teaching me other talents as well as those needed for film viewed by the general populace and he used the mother as a teaching tool, having me copy what he ordered the mother to do. It was presented to me as a normal way of life which I accepted although I didn't care for it.

I would stare at the occasional other child on the sets with me, eating the nasty cereal product and wonder if they smiled at home when ordered to swallow something they didn't want to, and were required to be sure to lick up every last drop by a demanding father figure. They must have been, wasn't everyone? I longed to talk with them about it but the father and the mother kept very close watch over me, guarding their darling paycheck.

By my sixth year I was already quite an accomplished reader. I had to be—it was part of my job. I dreamed of being Matilda, Roald Dahl's young hero, spent time fantasizing about wreaking vengeance on the parents. I had begun to explore reading material other than the endless scripts pushed at me and the occasional book (like MATILDA) given me as gifts from fans. Over the years I found there were a number of diverse choices in the parent's bedroom drawers and cupboards. I had the run of the house as long as I didn't try to leave the house. There were the usual (I thought) collections of naked bodies in every conceivable position (and some implausible to many), while in the living room book shelves there were what the parents considered tamer fare.

Carefully placed there, I'm sure to impress visitors, because I never saw the parents dipping into any of them. At about age 12 one book in particular grabbed my still fairly clean slate of a mind. I was a guest of my 'on set tutor', Shannon Toluene to a near by flea market, We were shooting an outdoor scene and the usually cooperative California sunshine suddenly ducked behind an ominous collection of gray, then black clouds. Since we would be forced to wait until it cleared, Shannon wanted to run over to a flea market she had passed by on her way in to the day's filming. The parents were afraid it would rain (a distressing thought for Californians and filmmakers working on location, and they sent me off in Shannon's care. They were not concerned about me melting; they didn't consider me made of sugar. I loved the flea market; I had a pocket full of single dollar bills and was among crowds of people who were more interested in used record albums, car parts and old paperback books, than in my minor celebrity. As Shannon was haggling over some 'Precious Moments' figurines, I spotted it—It was a thick maroon diary, very old, but seeming in good condition, embossed with the name of LIZZIE ANDREW BORDEN. It was dated back in 1880; twelve years before the infamous murders that had made Lizzie Borden a household name, it seemed to be written by the alleged murderess herself. I don't know if it was a legitimate diary, but it seemed to my lonely twelve year old self to be so, and I readily paid my $2.00 and tucked it, along with a purchase of a gaudy collection of jewelry, a bag full for $4.00 more, into Shannon's large backpack, labeled "Flea Market Finds" in her clever embroidery. I retrieved my treasures after filming finally finished for the day, the sun having reappeared and took it home, and read and reread it avidly, zipping through it in 2 days and nights, while hiding it away in plain sight on the shelves of books placed there for visitor effect.

There is something so compelling about dipping into another's diary, drinking deep of their thoughts, hopes and dreams. It was irresistible, to me, absolutely true and I began to feel very strong ties to the so called "ax murderess of Fall River". I knew how she felt—I too was trapped in an intolerable situation with two people who behaved in a manner I had no desire to be a party to. There was a great deal of money sitting somewhere in a bank from all the work I had done over the years, supposedly just waiting for me, but being enjoyed by these people who claimed to be my parents.

The early diary entries let me know that I had much in common with Lizzie. Evidently her uncle, John Vinnicum Morse (MY last name!), brother of Lizzie's late mother, had been a frequent visitor to the Borden home since his sister's death when Lizzie was two years old. It seemed that Uncle John felt it his duty to school young Lizzie as I had been taught by the man who called himself my father. Lizzie did not care for this conduct back then, any more than I did now. She had entries chronicling not only Uncle John's unwanted attentions, but similar visits by the family physician and friend of her fathers; Dr Bowen, who lived across the street. Lizzie felt there was no respite for her, if Uncle John was not making his frequent family visits to, as he put it "check up on my favorite niece" it was Dr. Bowen making a 'house call' to check on young Lizzie. Lizzie felt certain that her father had a good idea what was going on, but he didn't seem in any hurry to put a halt to things, so Lizzie felt it must be a normal way of life, although her sister Emma never seemed to have these lengthy visits with Uncle John or Dr. Bowen.

My heart stood still as I read these words. The diary sat in my lap; it felt hot to my touch—Lizzie had gone through the same situation I was living through now, only it had happened just over a hundred years ago! Was this the way life was supposed to be? Were adults meant to use young children in a way that was so degrading and hurtful to the spirit, or were Lizzie and I just two unfortunate souls who happened to have ended up in the same cosmic boat?

Lizzie went on to write of how she had gone to her father about the horrible situation one morning when Dr. Bowen had been unusually rough with her during one of his 'health checks ups', she was 30 years old now, why in God's name was the doctor still making these calls? Was this some time of eternal punishment? Lizzie told her father that she was going to tell the pastor of their church about the things that went on when the doctor or Uncle John visited. Maybe, she stated, she would tell the police constable too! Her father knew Lizzie had a temper and now that she was older, just might do such a thing, so Andrew suddenly countered with a suggestion- Lizzie might enjoy a holiday—England perhaps, "a breath of fresh air where she could think things through, young ladies must behave as their elders instructed them, but perhaps it is time for some time away from Fall River." Lizzie jumped at the chance to get away from the situation at home and joyfully packed for her 'new adventure' putting her anger away for now.

I particularly now noted a passage in which Lizzie wrote of her visit to 'the continent' and a meeting with, as she wrote it "a gentleman of color" Lizzie waxed poetic in her feelings for this mystery man; "The musician has ebony skin that is a dazzling breath of midnight in the noonday sun, his music speaks to me. As his fingers dance across the keys, the notes waltz into my heart. His eyes locked with mine and I felt him reading the loneliness and pain my soul possesses, soothing my battle scars with each resonant chord." Lizzie went on to say this man showed her "the true meaning of love and life— how to love and be loved, two spirits in exquisite harmony" Lizzie also wrote of a "'situation' that would have to be remedied once she returned to Fall River, but was well worth the risk, come what may."

I loved the prudential phrasing, having long been a lover of poetry, and could easily read between the lines, discovering an unknown fact. —MISS Lizzie Borden was

NOT a spinster lady as had always been recorded-not exactly. In the eyes of the populace of Fall River Miss Lizzie Borden was returning home as pure as she had left, but she had known this mystery man in a carnal sense, most unfitting a lady traveling alone in the late 1800's and was now figuring out what to do with a surprise package she would be bringing home. I was discovering what an excellent conniver Miss Lizzie was. How could she ever hope to hide this condition under her father's fraudulent puritanical eye? She believed that her father suspected, but this was simply not something one spoke of, it would ruin her father's good name in the community (which, Elizabeth noted with a smile, seemed to rather excite Lizzie) and about eight months after arriving home Lizzie again took a trip, this time to Rochester, New York for an open ended stay with supposed friends from her visit abroad over the summer. Evidently the surprise package arrived and was placed in May of the year 1881.

And here, I began to unravel another mystery—the mystery of Elizabeth Ann Morse. In my wanderings through the bookshelves and Ancestors.com I learned about my great, great grandfather—he had been adopted in 1881 by the Rochester Morse's, cousins of Andrew Borden's first wife, Sarah Morse. Although the neighbors were told that he was the bastard son of the housemaid, who had died in childbirth—(things were simply not shared publicly in those days it seems) although I imagine there were probably quite a few innuendos whispered at the sight of a Caucasian woman pushing a dark skinned baby around in a perambulator. Lizzie didn't seem to care about the gossip. I felt like a young Nancy Drew, digging up pieces that I realized constructed the puzzle of my beginnings. My great, great grandfather was christened Samuel Andrew Borden Morse and he in turn, years later, fathered my great grandfather Borden-Morse. I loved tracing the family back to the 1880's and even more important, discovering that I was a direct descendant of the infamous Lizzie Borden of the legendary sing song rhyme; "Lizzie Borden took an axe—gave her mother 40 whacks, when she saw what she had done she gave her father 41!"

Tracing the family tree further, through books and records in the bookshelves and the wonder of the computer, which I was rather adept at using, I discovered that another son had been born—this time to Samuel, who remained a bachelor until he was 50, at which time, in 1930, he married a Caucasian woman of 23 in order to carry on the family name. She finally became pregnant and delivered him a son, Jackson Samuel Borden Morse in 1935. Evidentially Jackson, who became a pharmacist, and quite the ladies man, made a great deal of money by coming up with some very popular drugs around 1960, including many for recreational use, and it was a very ripe era for that stock in trade. By 1970 Jackson had mad quite a fortune, dropped the Borden bit of the last name and a moved to San Francisco.

While plying his trade in that city of golden dreams, Jackson managed to impregnate many young women—it seemed this was his business as well as supplying drugs. One of these young women gave birth to a daughter who was given the name of Starlight Sunshine Morse. Starlight's mother was never legally married to Jackson, but they lived together until Jackson's death from an overdose of his own pharmaceuticals in 1979, leaving Starlight and her mother, who had adopted the name Fontana (in honor the sight where her daughter had been conceived one late night in Haight Ashbury) to make their own way. It was a wake up call for Fontana Morse, who decided keep Jackson's last name, but to leave San Francisco and travel back towards the east coast she had fled several years before.

With Starlight on her back, papoose style, Fontana finally ended up in Massachusetts. Funny how lives travel in a circle isn't it? Soon it was 1991 and Fontana and Starlight were at odds—as most mothers and daughters are at some point.

Starlight was 18 and a free spirit, unlike what she thought her mother had been. Fontana had taken a job with a small firm that became a big firm. The company grew taking Fontana the receptionist along until she became Fontana the customer service rep par excellence' and eventually, Ms.F.Morse, a minor vice president. Starlight ran off with her boyfriend, a 'no goodnik' according to what I could find on him, and in 1993 produced me—handing me over to the people who now claimed to be my parents. They were, evidently, a not very successful theatrical couple who had attempted to make it as actors in New York and failing were on their way to the west coast with dreams of Hollywood stardom; they came across Starshine, lugging a 5 month old daughter and begging. For $200.00 they purchased a new addition that might help pay their way to the bright lights of Hollywood, the father had an idea and Starshine did not want the responsibility of a baby. Done deal—no questions asked

Why me, that's what we all ask sometimes isn't it? Why would my so called birth mother give me away, could life have been so bad she couldn't live up to the responsibility she had after all, created for herself; and even then, when it had happened, why to THEM?

The so called PARENTS, who only took me as a means to an end, there was never any love or need involved, other than a need for something which took my childhood away and gave them a healthy profit, as well as allowing them to indulge their own perverse needs, while turning me into that which I am, whatever that is.

Then there is the coincidence of me finding the diary, but, does it really exist, coincidence? Or is it just us having a need to explain what we really make happen by our own hand.

Why did I of all people find Lizzie's diary? I still like flea markets, feel compelled to stop if I spot one, but why on that day, did I pick up that leather bound volume, and when I did, why did it immediately feel like I had to have it, almost as if it were mine, and simply being returned to where it had always belonged; and the two dollars I paid for it, seems like a small price doesn't it, for something that changes your life, or in fact defines it, gives it shape, makes it become what I suppose it was always meant to.

I was able to piece my beginnings and the tie to Lizzie Borden, beginning with Lizzie's diary then, letters and release of maternity forms, following the trail to my birth mother. I found no official adoption papers though—guess I was just a deal made with cash and a handshake. The computer and a credit card are very handy things when one wants information—and I wanted the information—this was my past, present, and my future, and defiantly, I decided—my destiny.

I decided that Miss Lizzie's only mistake—the thing that stopped an accident of pent up rage from becoming a grand career—was poor timing. I would not make the mistake my great, great grandmother had. I did not care to end up a recluse and then, there was the age difference. Lizzie had lived in a time when proper, good little girls 'shut up and put up' as he father had chastised me to do so many times. Lizzie had held on until she was 32 years old and they continued to take advantage, at least they thought they could until that hot August day when Uncle John showed up for one of his surprise visits. Lizzie, now that she 'had known real love and all that went with it', finally decided to take a stand. Lizzie told Uncle John to "go find someone else to toy with, she wasn't a doll to be taken advantage of any longer!"

Amazingly, Uncle John chose to slink away into the night air. Lizzie soon realized that the coward had chosen to creep to her father and whine about her behavior—she found out the next morning after an unappetizing start with the milk that Mrs. Borden complained had 'gone bad' and Mr. Borden's comment "that's not all that's gone bad" accompanied by a stern look at Lizzie. Mrs. Borden went upstairs to lie down after her stomach rebelled at the spoilt milk.

Mr. Borden then decided to read Lizzie the riot act about refusing her uncle his wishes, he raged for about 20 minutes on her duty to the family, then stormed into the study to give Lizzie time to, as he phrased it; "reconsider her use to this family—you owe a lot to your mother and me."

I envisioned Lizzie, holding her tongue with difficulty, ever the proper daughter. But Lizzie had finally had enough—without even thinking, she made her way down to the cellar and found the axe, climbed determinedly up the back stairs to where Mrs. Borden was making up the guest room bed and let her anger be known; showing just what she owed her step mother—whacking with all her might at the back of Mrs. Borden's head, quietly, but oh, so effectively. Lizzie wrote in her diary of "how freeing the act was—like a wild bird that had been trapped and caged, suddenly finding freedom". But one taste did not satisfy this wild bird; Lizzie craved yet more of the feeling, so she headed back downstairs to the study where father lay with his back to her on the settee, feet carefully off the floor as he slumbered. Lizzie walked stealthily up to him, and with the comment; "I HAVE reconsidered—my family's use to ME!" and took another whack—at her fathers head this time, rejoicing in the abrupt slump as her father's strength left his body, the blood oozing out of his skull in a welcome flood, and in the silence, she continued to hammer away, making certain she had completed her task, then went to change out of her blood soiled gown, the cornflower blue fabric now a dark, wet maroon, and then to clean herself up a bit. It was as if it was a daily chore, mastered at long last and she felt quite calm. Lizzie took the axe out to the barn, hid it away after cleaning it too and proceeded back to the house, where she came upon the remains of her father, as if it were a nightmare. She hollered for Bridget who was supposedly washing the windows, to "get help, someone has come into the house and killed father!" Then waited to see what would happen next. It was all, Lizzie wrote, "Rather like a dream unfolding or an engrossing book, and she was anxious to see what would happen next."

What happened next was very interesting. Dr. Bowen was called for; he took one look at the carnage and turned to Lizzie with a frightened look. "Who has done such a thing?" he asked her.

Lizzie looked him straight in the eye and replied, "Who do YOU think it could have been doctor? I wonder if they are still around and if anyone else could be marked for death?" she said calmly.

From that moment on, the good doctor was a staunch supporter of poor Miss Lizzie—from afar—encouraging the constable in saying "such forceful blows could not have been produced by a woman." The rest of the trial is, of course history, and I studied that history with interest, drawing conclusions and comparing it with the not so distant trial of O.J. Simpson, who was also acquitted of the charges of double murder. They had both been found Not Guilty, although the popular consensus seemed to be that both WERE guilty. I found that many believed my great great grandmother was acquitted by virtue of being a woman and that O.J. because he was an African American celebrity. The more I thought about it, the more certain I became. It was my destiny to follow in my great great grandmother's footsteps. I had so much in my favor. I am a female, I have an African American heritage from way back and I am a minor celebrity, thanks to the wonderful world of commercials and films, AND one more plus—I am only 13 years old. The last entry in Lizzie's diary seemed to speak from beyond the grave:

JO ANNE ALGIERS & RICHARD ANSELL

"If you cannot get rid of the family skeleton, you may as well make it dance" —George Bernard Shaw

I decided to make that skeleton dance, and dance until it dropped of exhaustion.

CHAPTER TWO
~The Plan~

At this point, I knew I had to begin planning; I would not commit an act out of pure rage—I would let it simmer as I planned. I made a list, my murder 'to do' list; I included what I would need and who I would need, not as accomplices per se; they would never know they were a part of THE PLAN.

Cash or money, safely stored in the bank or elsewhere, of my own, in my own name. One never knows when one need to leave in a hurry and readily available cash would be a definite plus.

Latex gloves – I intended to leave nothing that might lead back to me.

Alternate identities – being in the acting industry, I felt I could take care of this with no problem, but I wanted to plan them out, get to know them, breathe them, taste them, I guess there is a bit of the method actress in me.

Set a time line – I wanted the parents gone, but I needed to set the ground work. I decided on a 4 year limit to their lives.

Rehearsal…"Repetition on is the key to success" Success was the only acceptable outcome. Success was a NECESSITY!

I decided to use Shannon as my first accomplice. Shannon Toluene, my on—set tutor, the woman who had, unknowingly introduced me to my destiny, Shannon was a thityish, mousey young woman who wanted not only to impart wisdom, but to plant a seed of friendship, the reason for the flea market, I'm sure. I knew I could take advantage of Shannon's generous nature. We went to several other flea market outings—the parents considered her harmless. I accepted her offers of camaraderie, let her feel she was making a difference in my life, oohed and aahed over her little gifts of homemade taste treats (not difficult to do, Shannon was an excellent chef), let her feel she was special, important in my life, Shannon proudly wore the multi colored seed necklace I had found that first time at the flea market, and gifted her with to repay her kindness. The parents trusted her; Shannon didn't really trust the parents – even better. I began asking her for make up tips (something she obviously knew nothing about, but tried to impart her limited knowledge of) I joined in 'girl talk' with her (I actually began to enjoy it),

Shannon also imparted a special knowledge to me, one she never realized she taught me. Shannon Toluene was a student of 'the new age' she would go off into her private world of chants and astral planes while I was busy on the set and it fascinated me—I expressed am interest and through Shannon learned to separate myself from the unpleasant activities the parents insisted on. When the unwanted sexual encounters reared their ugly heads—I would go to my quiet place, my white room—located deep within myself. I no longer felt the physical pain or the emotional lashings to my spirit. For this, I was truly thankful to Shannon, it has stood me in good stead over the years and I was sorry to see her go—but, I could not deviate from 'the plan'. I kept up my friendship with Shannon for about three years, she saw me through 2 films and a television pilot that never flew. I managed to talk her into posing as my guardian, a sort of 'lets sneak around and pull one over on the grown ups' sort of thing, so that I could open my own personal bank account, siphoning money into it was a challenge, the parents didn't part with my money easily, so I foraged through their wallets and pocketbooks—they always had a healthy personal stash, and I could always get money from the frequent 'guests' they invited in for sexual games—I never recalled what happened while I was in 'my white room', enjoying my mental escape, but I had no qualms about taking their money.

My fifteenth birthday coincided with the finish of a film. There was invariably a 'wrap party' at the close of a film and I felt I was ready for a rehearsal for my Grandma Lizzie's Life of crime. I had poured over the diary for the past three years, studying, immersing myself in what I wished to accomplish. I realized that in order to reach my ultimate goal—the demise of the parents—some sacrifices would have to be made. Shannon was the first sacrifice.
I begged the parents to let me go to Shannon's home for a pool party the day after the wrap party. I knew I would have to pay the price that night for the next day's freedom, but it had to be done. I went through the motions with the parents AND the agent that night. He had been invited over for what they all felt was a well deserved sexual game. I, of course went into auto pilot when they began their disgusting intro to one of their ridiculous scenarios. The mother was told to dress herself and me in matching outfits and come to the 'Special Guest Room', a well padded room down below the huge house that the parents had had built with MY earnings. Whenever I heard mention of The Special Guest Room it was my queue to become the docile obedient child they had beaten into me over the years…

That night, the mother chose matching cherry red suits for us, as if we were going on an interview. She groomed me carefully, hair and makeup totally inappropriate for a young girl—but perfect for a young whore, I thought.

I let my mind go to my white room, where I thought through what I needed to do the next day with Shannon, and woodenly went through the adults play acting that the men were big time agents and the mother was willing to do ANYTHING to get her child a role in their film. I suppose they thought it was an art imitating life scenario—to me it was just sick. I'll leave the rest to your imagination—I was a mannequin in my white room as they directed my body in their disgusting game.

I thought only of my own plans, I regretted having to lose Shannon's friendship—but there are always casualties in a battle, and I was about to begin my war.

The next day, Shannon picked me up at 9:00 a.m. I had my swimsuit, latex gloves, a clean towel and a very large, very sharp knife stowed in a beach bag. The parent's saw us off with fake kisses and calls of "Have a great day!" and we were off. Shannon's home was in the hills about an hour away, it was a lovely drive in her BMW. But my mind was elsewhere. I had to work within THE PLAN. We arrived at Shannon's home, a comfortable 'beach house' though built into the side of a hill. Her swimming pool was an indoor pool, not too large, but big enough to cool off and relax while I thought things through. We had a late breakfast of Shannon's homemade omelets with fresh mushrooms, bacon and basil from her window herb garden. I helped with the prep and set the little glass dining table with her bright red placemats, my favorites, noting the wonderful contrast to the colorful fiesta ware. Once we had eaten, over Shannon's protests I insisted on clearing, and wiping the table, then loading the dishwasher and running it. I did not want to leave my fingerprints on anything. She changed into her swimsuit, chatting away and Shannon headed to the pool, I said I would be right behind her. And I was. When I came to the pool Shannon was sitting on the steps, arms bent, leaning on her elbows, her short sassy red hair wet and gleaming. She must have dived in and come back to this perfect position to wait for me. I paused, admiring the convenient pose. As if had been rehearsed, I walked silently and calmly behind her with my shining knife and cut straight across her throat. It was very quiet, though her eyes screamed out, asking 'why'? They then suddenly took on a glazed 'out to lunch forever' look. I stood and just looked at what I had wrought, the knife dripping Shannon's ruby remnants into the pool. The silence was hanging heavy in the air. She hadn't made a sound; there had just been a short of gurgle as I looked curiously down into her startled, then empty blue eyes. I hadn't wanted to hurt or frighten her, she had been of use to me and rather kind, but Shannon Toluene's usefulness was over and I needed to move forward with THE PLAN. I was wearing the latex gloves I had brought along so I began my clean up. The Plan danced thru my mind – tidy up, no fingerprints, no signs that I was ever here, I proceeded to the dishwasher and put one set of dishes, silverware and my orange juice glass back where they belonged. In so doing I passed by her computer and a thought exploded in my head. I had to get it down. Still wearing my latex gloves I logged on to her computer, the trusting soul had shared her password with me—I went to her word page and typed the words that were buzzing sp insistently at me:

SCARLET RUBIES, YOUR FINAL JEWELS OF DEATH
FADING, LIQUFIED WITH YOUR FINAL BREATH
SHELL NOW SO SERENE IN YOUR REPOSE
SOUL GENTLY SOARING, IN PEACE IT GOES

I retrieved a small hammer from Shannon's utility drawer and hammered the page neatly into the top of her skull. Then I just pushed the body into the warm pool water with my foot, watched the red smear the water a pale pink, then went and got my towel to clean up the little bit of blood that had dripped onto the pool deck.

When I was quite certain things were in order, I headed down the road on Shannon's mountain bike, I had ridden it in the film we had just finished and Shannon had purchased it from the prop department when filming wrapped. I enjoyed the freedom of the ride. Along the way, when I came to a quiet spot, I found a trash can and tossed my towel inside with a match from Shannon's kitchen utility drawer, made sure it was burning totally then resumed the ride. When I was about 2 miles from the parent's home I ditched the bike and strolled to the park near the parent's home, sat reading The Diary, which was always with me. At about 4:00 I walked home, stopping by the corner news stand to buy a copy of VARIETY. Two days later we saw the terrible news of Shannon Toluene's death on the evening news and I wept convincingly and skipped dinner.

I was moderately surprised at the ease of committing the necessary deed, I was perfectly calm before, during and after the act, for that was what it felt like—an act. I was able to distance myself and take care of business; I had learned that trick from Shannon, God bless her, and it came in handy when the abuse from the parents and the other adults in the world that encased me. I think finding my great, great grandmother's diary had been preordained for me. I began to think it had been planted for me to find so that I could release the parent's from their hell on earth; the vicious calling that forced them to perform such lewd acts upon my person and upon my psyche. Yes, that must be it—the diary was their invitation to me to deliver them, commute their sins in any way I cared to. I also decided that what they had done to me over and over throughout the years demanded harsh handling and I had now proved myself equal to the calling. I felt powerful for the first time in my 15 years; I was a voice to be reckoned with!

Was I unraveling? No, I was Becoming, I was on my way to

being who I was meant to be—before my birth mother had tossed me into the scarred clutches of these people who claimed to be my parents. I started at that time to think about my birth mother and how she was yet another adult who had stepped on my soul, squashed my inner spirit. I knew I would have to add her to THE LIST.

The parents were very upset when the news of Shannon's accident was televised; here was a crime that touched close to home in that they knew her well, I had been her student, been to her home, Of course the police had to question me as I had seen her so close to the date of the discovery of her wet corpse. No one, except the parents knew I had visited Shannon at her home, and they certainly had no desire to mention it. I knew the police would question us, we had seen her on the set that final day of filming. I was calm then too, I had many years of acting to fall back on, I was a pretty young girl, who would honestly believe that I could be involved? Sweet Elizabeth Anne Morse hammers a nail into the skull of her beloved tutor? Nah...

I replayed my day at Shannon's for the good looking policeman, Sgt. Greenspade, he said I could call him Harry, "not dirty Harry though," he commented, "that would be 'Doc', but you're not in big enough trouble to be talking to Doc." He grinned, I noticed the other officer sort of smirked at this stab at making me feel at ease and I decided the young cop was a newcomer that would be better off labeled Sgt. Greenhorn, he seemed such a novice. I recounted the day, having it end at about 3:30 with Shannon dropping me off at the corner near my house so that I could bring home a copy of VARIETY for the parents from the corner newsstand. Everything in order, everything well thought out, everything according to THE PLAN.

"Yes, I think we do still have the copy, we keep them all" I replied to Sgt. Harry, watching him watch me, studying me. I knew I was safe, I was invincible. I HAD made sure to stop in at the newsstand and get a copy of VARIETY, I HAD chatted for a moment with Sergio, the proprietor. I retrieved the copy of VARIETY from the stack in the corner of the den and I seated myself at the grand piano in our living room, I noticed Sgt. Harry admiring one of my smiling head shots framed on the top of the piano. "Would you like an autographed copy? We have a stack in the desk." Without waiting for an answer beyond his schoolboy blush, I rose, went to the desk and extracted one of the ridiculous glamour shots, writing: 'Best of luck Harry~ yours ~Elizabeth Morse—'and handed it to him.

He stood up and blushing even more, cleared his throat and motioned to the other officer. "Thank you Miss Morse. I think we have all we need from you right now." I swallowed my urge to laugh out loud at this star stuck fool, simply smiled, and went back to the piano as he turned away. This chapter was finished and I began to play softly as he walked out with the other officer, handing the parents his card "in case they thought of anything else".

I had taken to dipping into The Diary at every opportunity for I had noticed something unusual after the news of Shannon's "suspicious death" as the news called it. I came across a new entry in the diary. It was still in Lizzie's prim handwriting, but it was speaking of the recent events, as if Lizzie had proudly taken care of the necessity of relieving me of Shannon's presence. I read the new entry with surprised interest two days after the event: ~~AH, THE FEELING OF POWER AGAIN AND NO MORE HAVING TO HIDE BEHIND A MASK OF GENTILITY, SO REFRESHING. I AM ONCE AGAIN FEELING MY HEART SING~~ the entry went on to praise the smooth way that things had been carried out and I swelled with pride.

I knew that I shouldn't carry out the next step too soon, I would have to endure the parents for a while longer, but they seemed somehow subdued by the recent events, much as Uncle John and Dr. Bowen had been in Lizzie's case.

I found myself retiring to my mental white room more and more often. The business of acting is a squirming, slippery one—I had, in my fourteenth year, several commercials (toothpaste—my sparkling smile was glorious against my latte skin tones, ads for Polaroid cameras (for the same reason), Then in my fifteenth year I landed a couple of guest spots on LAW AND ORDER, of all things, where I met a charming advisor on police procedure, Lt. Zachary Murdock, (called simply 'Doc' by the crew)-his stunning smile and ever watchful brown eyes reminded me of someone, but I could not recall who—he intrigued me. I was playing the role of a teenaged counterfeiter who accidentally becomes involved with a murder, and would follow Doc as he discussed police procedure with the writers and director. He was so intelligent, well, as far as police procedure, and always had a smile and a friendly nod or wink for me, didn't seem to mind my eavesdropping on his conversations with the writers—in fact he sort of included me in the discussions even if it wasn't about my scenes.

CHAPTER THREE
~Lex Mungo~

All in all it was a slow year publicly, but the parents tried to make up for any monetary loss by pushing me into a couple of 'soft porn' features, directed and produced by their friend Lex Mungo, who had been a frequent 'guest' at their little 'get together'. I assumed he came up with that ridiculous moniker on his own, I'm sure he loved seeing it splashed across a big screen. After having me 'star' in 2 of his raunchy extravaganzas, Lex decided it was time for him to feature himself in one with me. When the parents made this announcement, toward my 16th birthday, my stomach turned over—Lex Mungo was a self centered, inconsiderate, over tanned and over plastic surgery enhanced loser who just happened to have money to throw around, most of it ill gotten, I was certain.

The parents stood with their pocketbooks open, their thoughts for my welfare negligible, as long as there was cash to be had.

As I poured over The Diary that evening, I took note of a new entry; Grandma Lizzie seemed to have awakened— THAT SCUM DOES NOT BELONG ON THIS EARTH. HIS KIND MUST BE DEALT WITH SEVERLY. I read it as if it was a schoolgirl note passed under the teachers watchful eyes. Surreptitiously memorizing the words, I closed The Diary and began to work on the new plan—The Lex Flex I called it in my head. The next morning I read in The Diary—I HOPE SHE WILL PREPARE AS CAREFULLY FOR THIS SCENARIO AS THE LAST, PERHAPS FEIGN EXCITEMENT AND REQUEST A REHEARSAL—THAT SHOULD APPEAL TO THE HORRIBLE MAN'S VANITY—THE LAST PAT ON HIS TOO TANNED SHOULDER—

I smiled and silently congratulated Lizzie on a brilliant idea. I asked the father to phone the conceited fool so that I could speak with him. I told him I wanted to be perfect for the shoot, saying I could tell he was so talented and I knew a rehearsal would be in my best interest...The father looked suspicious, but dialed the number—warning me not to make waves, and then repeated a phrase that had led to a man's demise, 100 years ago; "reconsider your use to this family— you owe a lot to your mother and me." I took the phone and demurely asked if we could please have a private rehearsal session before filming so that I could be perfect. I could practically see the arrogant fool salivating and preening as he agreed that "Yes, yes, that would be an excellent idea my dear" and that he would pick me up at 9:00 that night, we would be filming at a motel not too far away, in the valley. I noticed the father looking both pleased at my seeming acceptance of the inevitable and also a look of jealousy that he was not to be included. I practically skipped upstairs to gather and pack my 'things'—the parents picked out a skimpy, disgusting white baby doll nighty set that made my stomach turn, but I dutifully packed it, then told them I wanted to rest up for awhile. They left me and I packed my latex gloves, towel, a feather duster, the sharp knife and The Diary, I also included pair of handcuffs I had procured from the set of Law And Order and a syringe full of epinephrine we had for the mothers allergy to bee stings—you never know when something may come in handy. All packed and ready for whatever was to come I laid down to rest contentedly until 9:00.

At about 8:40 Lex Mungo arrived at the house to drive me to the 'rehearsal'. The father let him in, grudgingly—he knew which side his check was buttered on, but did not like to let someone else have control of his prize. Lex had such a stupid, almost drooling grin and a glazed look on his face as he accompanied me to the waiting car, trying desperately to make small talk. I sat quietly letting him prattle. "I have some really interesting ideas for the film, want to really let you stretch yourself honey, try some new things out, I hope you're open to trying new things tonight…" He was making me sick, trying to be a suggestive teenaged boy in his reworked physique and store bought tan. We pulled up at the LaZ-Time Motel and Lex practically flew out of the car, running around to open my door as if it was a newlywed and his bride on their honeymoon, that lust filled face beginning to sweat a bit, the old letch reached for my hand to lead me to his den of iniquity.

I patted his hand and said quietly, "Now Lex, are YOU ready to try something new? I am interested in something new and adventurous—will you let me take the director's chair? I want to prove I'm not just some dumb little girl, not just a puppet, how are YOU at following direction?"

The idiot was beside himself with eagerness, I saw his manhood bulging with the idea of me taking charge of his destiny tonight—good, and I was more than ready to write his finale'. He fumbled with the room key he had in his pocket— must have checked in BEFORE he picked me up, not wanting to be seen with an underage female—I smiled at his good planning. He pushed the door open ceremoniously, "What did you have in mind my dear? I can get the designers to come with your wildest dreams for filming, order any costumes — your wish is my command!" I smiled to myself — Lex was going to be putty in my hands. I walked slowly around the cheap motel room with its generic landscapes on the wall to compliment its non-exclusive bedspread covering 150 thread-count linen dreams, and the universal tawdry table and chairs.

"Well…I mused," running my fingers along his hairy forearm. "I've always wanted to do a period piece, be a princess in a tower at the mercy of the evil king." I saw his eyes sparkle and he licked his lips at the thought. "Maybe the little princess has long had an eye for the king," Lex's ego took the stroke and savored it as he followed me with his eyes, his erection growing with every word I spoke, I felt like Scheherazade, spinning my tale to keep the master captivated, "She has spent long nights under her father's watchful eye, alone in her castle tower room, dreaming of the rival king and his strong gait, his manly thighs strutting into her father's domain, and feels the need to have her ripe flower plucked before it dries and the beautiful bloom fades…" I was doing all I could not to laugh at my ridiculous storyline and the even more grotesquely lascivious gleam in the pedophile's eyes.

"Brilliant my sweet! You do know I was once an actor, don't you?" he stated stupidly through the haze of lust he was passing through on his way to my side. I put my hand on his chest to halt him.

"Let's try it, improvise the scene — I've taken improvisation classes, I'll set the scene and you follow my directions.

He bowed grandly, playing the game if it was going to lead up to his ravishing the fair maiden. "Very well, hmmm…the scene opens in the castle keep, the bedchamber of the princess. She enters to find her dream has come true! There is the vision of her fantasy, her fathers rival, sitting naked" at this point Lex began removing his clothes so fast I would have guessed he had discovered ants in his pants, "the well endowed king" (what a joke—he looked like all the rest of them) "is seated, legs proudly apart" He immediately sat in one of the cheap arm chairs and opened his legs—what an idiot the man was—"the princess discovers him, she is elated, but then she sees her dream lover is blindfolded," I rushed to the bathroom and grabbed a hand towel to tie around his face, then paused, slowly stripping off my own clothes as I did so, Lex's eyes grew larger and I could see the beads of sweat on his brow as I tied the towel over his eyes, I let my breasts rub across his face as I positioned the towel, keeping up my running dialog, "she is aghast to see he is also shackled" Lex chuckled eagerly as I put the handcuffs on him, securing his hands behind him and to the table, "the princess must comfort her kingly paramour, although she knows no way to free him," I began running the feather duster over his body, I could see he was aching with desire. I moved away and unzipped the other compartment of my bag, removing my latex gloves and the knife.

Lex grinned, sucking in some drool and commented, "I think the king needs more substantial attention."

I proceed to the chair with my knife and replied as I took his erect kingly member in my latex covered hand,"The princess approaches her lover, wanting to give him everything she has dreamed of giving him,"

"I hope he gets it soon, I'm about to erupt baby."

I continued, as I held his erection, "But what is this? It is her father!" and I took a healthy slice out of Lex's penis, carving away as he screamed and the blood flowed between his legs,

"You crazy bitch! What the hell are you doing?"

I continued, calmly; "No man shall deflower my daughter! Cries her father to his rival king, I will see him dead before he touches her" I ran the knife in a gleaming arc across his throat, watching the scene as if I were watching the dailies of a slasher movie, listening to Lex's incredulous gasping screams muffled by the rapid influx of blood, his placid body now slumped forward, arms lax and head at a curious angle.

I decided to leave the penis hanging by a tag of testicle as I asked the now silent child molester, "Was it good for you?" before I turned and went to shower. When I came back out, Lex was so done for, sitting in a pool of his own blood, his once proud penis hanging by a mere patch of testicle from his renovated torso. I was actually quite pleased with my performance, now that I had showered off every hint of the nasty beast having touched me and redressed. I took another look through the tawdry room, thinking that Lex's drained of life body was much more attractive than the animated one had been. I decided to further enhance him—I strolled quietly to the newsstand in the parking lot and purchased a newspaper, I had some time and manicure scissors so I cut out a farewell poem and attached it with nail polish, necessity being the mother of invention. I pasted it from his forehead down to his bloodied feet;

Lucifer's brother—No heart, no mother
Feasting on innocent spirit
Believing no one will hear it
Nirvana found in youthful souls bound
Knowing you're evil but burying the thought
Lust and your all mighty dollar sought
Now you see—Satan's been caught
Paid the piper-And he charged quite a lot!

It was very entertaining going through the paper, cutting out words and letters. The nail polish I had was a vibrant red, which I thought set off the picture quite well, sure to be a pleasant surprise for the cleaning staff. I put the remnants of newspaper neatly into the trash can outside, putting the DO NOT DISTURB sign on the door handle as I gathered my things and walked through the soon to be daylight to a bus stop up the street. I wore nondescript jeans and a gray sweat shirt with oversized, tinted glasses and a grey bandana to hide any parts of me that might be recognizable, pulling off the latex gloves only as I was sitting on the bus bench and putting them in my pocket. I boarded the bus just as the sun was rising over the smog filled valley, thinking that I had rid the world of at least one human pollutant. The bus took about 2 hours to get me to a stop near the house, all those stops really added time to the ride and gave me a chance to rest and go over my story for the parents. I planned on being very quiet, giving the impression that the situation had overwhelmed me, letting them surmises that I had bitten off more then I could chew. I would suggest that Lex had brought another woman along and insisted she join in, knowing the idea would both interest and anger the father—he liked to be thoroughly informed of things and would feel that he had been taken unfair advantage of…I strolled the block and a half to the house from the bus stop in a calm mood—mission accomplished.

 I was surprised to find the father pacing the living room floor as I entered. I felt like one of those 1950's sitcom family's as he demanded, "Well?"

 "Well what?" I replied as I set my overnight bag at the foot of the sweeping staircase.

 "Did you enjoy going out on your own? Leaving me behind?" The father sounded more like a jealous teenage boyfriend than the adult who abused me on a regular basis.

 "Actually, I wasn't on my own. Your friend Lex brought someone along." I saw the vein his forehead bulge. Not a particularly attractive sight.

 "He what? That son of a bitch, he didn't mention bringing anyone along!"

 "Maybe he doesn't tell you everything, I think it was just some whore he picked up somewhere, she didn't look familiar at all—not one of your regulars, I don't think…" The vein was really popping out now—maybe he would have some kind of attack and save me the trouble. "I'm tired; I'm going to go to sleep." I picked my bag back up and climbed the stairs to my bedroom, wondering what the next move would be. I made it almost to my room before the father came galloping up the stairs.

"Was he that good? Wore you out? I'll show you 'worn out' you little tramp!" The father grabbed my arm and threw my bag into the bedroom; he ripped my sweatshirt off of me and tossed it after the bag, "you want to be worn out?" He was yanking my jeans down and when they were around my ankles he pushed me to the floor of the hallway, half in, half out of my room. He was unbuckling his own jeans in preparation, when I lifted my feet off of the floor and shoved against his chest, knocking him back onto his ass. I was NOT in the mood for his male ego to take its vengeance, maybe I had finally found my inner strength through these tasks I had set myself, perhaps it was the spirit of my great great, grandmother taking control, but I was NOT going to be attacked by this disgusting excuse for a guardian! We lay there, both halfway out of our respective pants, I was feeling ready to fight—the father looked ready to just turn to stone, he was so incredulous, I had NEVER refused his advances before although I had always wanted to.

We had reached an impasse and just stared at each other for a moment. I thought about how an animal trainer on the set of one of my films, had once told me—"stare the animal down—whichever of you breaks eye contact first has given up the showdown" I was not going to lose—ever again. The father looked away. I didn't budge as he stood and pulled his jeans back up and re buckled his belt. Without another word or look, he walked back downstairs. I sat for another minute, savoring my victory and saying to him under my breath, "Go fuck yourself."

I'm not sure how long I sat there relishing the sweet flavor of victory, eventually; I rose, pulling my jeans back up and slammed the door-an action to put an exclamation mark on the end of the scene. I opened my bag and double checked my supplies for cleanliness, I would return the knife to the kitchen later, and it would be a secret source of amusement to watch the parents using it to slice meat for their sandwiches with the same instrument that had carved out Lex and Shannon's final moments.

CHAPTER FOUR
~Investigation~

    Not another word between the father and me, the mother had obviously not been told a thing about what had transpired; we simple kept a watchful silence, the mother watching the father and the father shadowing me with his angry glances as I watched the two of them.
    It took about 4 days for the murder at the LaZ Time to hit the air. Police were, according to news reports "On the lookout for an as yet unknown assailant in the brutal slaying of 62 year old Lex Mungo, film producer. Mr. Mungo's body had been found by a cleaning woman. It is uncertain just how long the body had been there, there had been a 'Do Not Disturb' sign on the door for at least 48 hours according to the management."
    The parents were in a panic mode, they held clandestine meetings where trepidation was the overall mood. I stayed in

the living room listening to frenzied whisperings as they attempted to come up with a way that neither what they considered their good name, nor I—their meal ticket, would be dragged through the mud. They would start out in a very low, secretive tone and within minutes I was listening to "We can't let it get out!" "She'll ruin us!" "You never should have let her go!" "What, like you were trying to stop her—you didn't want to make the money?" It was comic how frightened they were, I decided to add to their fright a bit so I commented as though thinking aloud; "I should let the police know about that other woman that was there…" My comment was greeted by a resounding unison of "NO!" as the two came rushing over to me.

The father grabbed me roughly by the shoulders and shook me as he said through clenched teeth "You will NOT say anything about being anywhere near that place!"

I looked at him innocently and replied "But it might help with the investigation."

The mother looked at me as if I were aiming a gun at her heart, "What it might help with is ending your career forever! We've invested years in you young lady, you will not throw it all in the trash heap!"

The father looked approving at this assessment, "Right—you will not say a thing about where you were or what went on, or anything that ever went on concerning Lex."

"Or concerning us!" the mother added.

"But what if…" I began, hoping to further antagonize them.

The father gripped me again "What if nothing. You were never there and only knew MR. Mungo from the film sets he was a producer on. You didn't even know his first name. Got it?" he demanded, his fingers squeezing my upper arms so tightly, I was sure I would have bruises.

I broke loose and looked at him with a typical teenager to parent scowl, "Yes! Geez, bruise me for life, why don't you?

Of course we won't even worry about any fingerprints or that DNA crap, why should we?"" I said in a tone of voice to match the scowl as I scooped up The Diary off of the sofa and headed to my room, a smirking grin on my face once my back was turned. I could almost feel them sweating.

It was another week before the authorities came knocking at the door. The parents were both basket cases every time they flipped the on the television and saw another update on the 'grizzly scene in the LaZ Time Motel": as the newscasters would invariably announce it, or there would be a knock at the door. When it finally came, I was the one to answer the knock and to my surprise saw Lt. Murdock and another officer on the doorstep. He greeted me with the same grin he had on the set. "Good morning Elizabeth, may we speak to your parents please?"

"They're not my real parents and of course you may," I answered with my own smile as I opened the door fully and added, "You look better without a cast" referring to the broken arm he had had, which had been the reason he was acting as a technical support person for Law and Order the weeks I was filming it. The two officers, Lt. Murdock in plainclothes and the other my old friend 'Not dirty Harry Greenspan,' in uniform, but still blushing like crazy, stepped in as the parents came rushing out, trying to look casual.

"Sorry to disturb you, we need to ask a few questions of anyone who knew Mr. Lex Mungo, just routine," said Lt. Murdock with that dazzling smile. I decided to jump right in and start the parent's nerves fraying.

"Mr. Mungo? The producer? I always liked him so much; he was very attentive to my needs, wasn't he?" I pointed this question toward the father, who suddenly seemed a bit pale.

"So you knew him Elizabeth?" Lt. Murdock nodded with a slightly raised brow to Sgt. Harry, who had pulled a small notebook out and was busily scratching away.

The mother decided to save the day and cut in with, "Of

course she knew him—we all did, he produced two of Elizabeth's films; RUNAWAY and PINK PROMISES, both were big hits, and I must admit made Mr. Mungo a pretty penny, not that Elizabeth didn't get her fair share of the profits—he made sure she did and of course he usually hosted a celebration when the filming was completed and another when each film premiered, he was a very generous man, Lex Mungo..." the mother was rambling on, desperate to keep me from saying anything damaging.

Doc was watching her with what looked to me like amusement, he finally broke into the mother's barrage of information with, "Yes, the premieres of those two films—there is footage of Elizabeth at the premieres on the arm of Mr. Mungo..." and he pulled out a glossy 8x10 of me clinging to Lex's arm.

The father turned paler still and seemed to be sorting through mental storage cabinets for a valid sentence to explain the photo of a 14 year old girl hugging tight to a 60 year old man. The mother's eyes were like a deer in headlights. I decided to ply my trade; after all, I did make my living as an actor. "Oh! That was my first big premiere, I don't know who was more afraid—me or Mr. Mungo of losing his money!" I gave a little chuckle and the parents visibly relaxed. "Things were a lot easier when the film was a hit, at least for Mr. Mungo; I still had to do all those talk shows..."

Doc smiled and commented, "I imagine so..." to me, while still watching the parents. "Then you had no contact with Mr. Mungo outside of business?" This was addressed to the parents, but I chimed in a comment to keep them nervous.

"Oh, but he came by here sometimes," I added helpfully. The father gave me an annoyed hairy eyeball, the mother glanced around as if the body of Lex would saunter in soon.

"He would come by on studio business, papers to sign, contract options to discuss, he really did lookout for his investments." The father smiled at Doc in a 'man to man' sort of way, inferring there was nothing that I would have understood involved.

"But Elizabeth was aware of what was happening to her – career wise? She seems a very mature and capable young lady to me." I wanted to kiss Doc for scoring a point for my team— no one ever spoke up for me, made me sound like I knew what was going on in my life. "Or was she just another of his investments?" This question stopped the father cold—I wanted to kiss the Doc yet again—this was one smart man, he defiantly read between the lines. An investment, a product— was exactly how the parents and all of their so called friends viewed me. I could see by the parent's faces that they could perceive the direction the Doc's thoughts were going.

The mother jumped right in, without thinking obviously, "She's just a kid—she wouldn't be interested in all the business end of things. She's fed and dressed, what else does she need? We're the one's that have to keep everything going" She sounded a little miffed and the father was not at all pleased with her speaking up.

The father gave a slight chuckle, as if to now discount his wife's opinion, "Of course, whenever Elizabeth has a question about any business matters she knows she can come right to me—I'll answer any questions she puts to me." He now shot the mother a withering glare, to me, a poorly executed fatherly nod and the police officers another manly smile and wink. He received nothing back from any one.

Doc looked from one to the other of us, measuring things, analyzing comments and body language and, I believed, storing impressions for later perusal. I trusted the man, assumed he was, somehow an allied soul. He nodded to the other officer, who closed his little notebook, and handed Doc out two business cards, one he gave to the parents, one to me, "Well then, I think that's all we need for now. Please feel free to call if you think of anything that might have bearing on the investigation" this was to the parents, then to me, "Or if you just need to talk." And I swear he winked at me.

CHAPTER FIVE
~Doc~

I winked at her, yeah, but I was just letting her know I was on her side. I had seen these show business babies before—dragged down and sucked dry by the greedy adults that claimed to care for them, then left high and not at all dry, but soaked in debt while the greedy grown ups spent the kids earnings. This one I had pegged when I did some time on the set of Law and Order, while I was on paid leave, having wound up with a clipped wing after chasing after a Hollywood pimp who disagreed with my assessment of his business dealings. He ended up in prison for not enough years, I ended up in a cast and as technical advisor for the 'cop wannabe's', all in all a fair trade off. I had earned my detective status on that collar, and a reputation as a champion of innocents—something I must have picked up from my military upbringing. "Leave no man behind" had been drummed into me from the get go. I had always been the refuge for the put upon, the bully's choice targets found their way under my wing and it continued once I joined the police force. I, of course began my stint in the streets of Los Angeles—they start you off where life is the toughest, I suppose to see what you're made of. –I like to think that I'm made of a diamond—beautiful to look at and unbreakable, except when it comes to the underdog—the one with 3 strikes against them that keeps swinging away. When I come across them I step up to the bat, and sometimes hit the bad guy over the head with it. That pimp had been one of the bad guys and I thought I saw the same glint in the eyes of these 'guardians' who I thought were mainly guarding their own interests.

Elizabeth Ann Morse was a cup of sweet latte, sugar and spice—she had probably never really had the chance to be a kid, or be WITH other kids, she had the usual over watchful Hollywood parents—a matched set for Elizabeth, father and mother hovering around the paycheck, keeping an eye and an ear on everything Elizabeth said or did. She somehow reminded me of a couple of the street kids that had hung around the low spots I had checked out when I would sneak out of my theatre classes at RADA, cutting off my nose to spite my reflection—I never was much on rules and regulations, having grown up in a military world, my father was a Marine Corps guard at the American Embassy in the U.K, met my mother while on duty (mum's father was in the British Embassy and a frequent visitor to the American building) and as the story goes—the meeting of my folks was Kismet. Thus, I was blessed with dual citizenship and spent my childhood dragged back and forth across the pond as Dad's orders dictated. We finally settled in the U.S. and I ended up in a military school, and then talked the folks into RADA when I showed a flair for the stage. Mum was thrilled at the thought of my being back in London and it started out alright, couldn't stand being trapped in class, though I did enjoy the rehearsals and performances, met a few great girls when I was cast in

JO ANNE ALGIERS & RICHARD ANSELL

TAMING OF THE SHREW—I guess Petruchio is a real charmer, I however found the allure of the casinos more intriguing than the call of the spotlights and applause—figured I would make a quick killing at the tables then head back to the U.S. I'm glad Chance stepped in to my life and pointed me toward the police force—my folks are too, they had about given up on me.

But, I didn't care for what I was seeing here. Elizabeth was being used, I didn't know quite how, either emotionally, physically, sexually—but this one was being used. I could see it in her eyes, feel it in her movements. Something was going on here and I was going to find out what, and do something to set things straight. I knew a little of what it was like to be pigeon holed and made to do things you really didn't care to. It probably had nothing to do with Lex Mungo, but I was going to dig around—I'm a cop, a detective—it's what I get to do.

Interesting thing about people with guilty consciences, they over explain things. You don't even have to ask a question and they are answering what they are afraid of you asking, except the young ones—they cover for the adults, telling you what you are after by saying the opposite. When Elizabeth and her guardians said Mungo had only been to their home 'on business' they gave me another avenue to explore, the fathers heartily glowing skin had said a lot too—the man had been silently sweating like a pig in the Phoenix summer heat, and only took his eyes off of Elizabeth for quick, pissed off glances at his wife's overkill of info. Something was defiantly worth exploring in this family. As I sat in my unmarked car, I made a decision, a decision I might regret later, but I decided to be Elizabeth Ann Morse's guardian angel—hell, the kid was due for a friend.

I did a little more digging into Lex Mungo's affairs—and there were certainly a lot of affairs to dig into—the man was a player from way back and followed a well worn path, one I might have ended up on if I had been stupid enough to stay on the acting trail. Chance had stepped onto my path, Mungo hadn't been so lucky. He was like a million other 'would be stars' he had had a few small movie roles in the 60's, nothing to speak of really, but he wouldn't accept that he wasn't made for the film business—Lex Mungo (whose real name I discovered was Leonard Montgomery), did like so many before him—made his bread by 'acting' in some porn films. Back in the 60's and 70's they were an exciting new genre' for struggling actors—Leonard had his name changed and became a darling of the X rated classics—then he found he could make even more money directing and producing the shit. Lex Mungo gave quite a few porn stars their step up from hooking and hustling to the 'film business', I could just imagine the creep enticing young Hollywood hopefuls from Ohio, Wisconsin and Idaho with stars in their eyes into the bowels of the business, it was no surprise to me that someone had decided to off the creep.

Now, I needed to follow the rope, unravel it to see where Elizabeth's folks came into contact with Mungo—and had he managed to pull Elizabeth along? I really hoped not—the young lady had somehow gotten under my skin, and it didn't happen often—I had become sort of immune to feminine wiles – I thought. But Elizabeth was different. She had not tried to 'fem' her way into my heart, she just seemed to be there, her essence seemed to have always been drifting through there and I had just finally discovered the source, the vessel. Sounds corny, I guess, but I felt as though I had discovered a missing piece of myself in her. And I was not about to see it destroyed.

I continued to delve into Elizabeth's guardians—they had adopted her name; Morse, as well as her person, bought and paid for 'under the table' so to speak. There was no official adoption paper, there didn't even seem to be an original birth certificate for Elizabeth, I went through all the usual routes but kept coming up short at brick walls, my Elizabeth seemed to have come out of nowhere—I decided to run some DNA through the usual channels, so headed back to the Morse household and asked, oh, so politely if I could have swabs of their saliva—just routine I explained, we're trying to eliminate you from the possible contacts I told them. Mr. Morse was not exactly happy to oblige, but he grudgingly opened for the uniformed officer to take and label a generous amount of his spit and drool after Elizabeth jumped right up and offered her open mouth. Mrs. Morse realized it would only make her look guilty to refuse, but I'm sure she would have liked to—there were skeletons hanging in that closet.

I sat down next to Elizabeth at the grand piano, she was playing Chopsticks softly as her guardians were giving their samples and exchanging nervous looks, and when I began to play a counterpart to the tune, her face lit up with a genuine smile, although she didn't look directly at me. "So you play?" she asked quietly, her eyes watching my fingers dance on the keys.

Smiling to myself I said, "I did in another life" and kept playing, Elizabeth suddenly giggled and lifted her hands from the keys.

"Bring it home!" she laughed, and I went into a swing time version of Chopsticks, which she seemed to love. I brought it to a crescendo, stood up and bowed to her enthusiastic applause, then collected the DNA swabs from the uniformed officer, told her guardians pointedly that I would be in touch, and headed back to headquarters.

CHAPTER SIX
~Lizzy~

I went back to my room and re read The Diary—again. I felt that there was something, somewhere that I was missing. I read from the end backward—there was a new entry that read: THINGS ARE GOING VERY WELL, SHE IS ON THE WAY TO THE FINAL GOAL, BUT MUSTN'T RUSH THINGS—WHAT GOES AROUND COMES BACK AROUND—AND WITH A VENGENCE. SHE JUST CANNOT TAKE THE WRONG CHANCE—THE WINDOW WILL OPEN WHEN THE TIME IS RIGHT.ONE MUST WATCH FOR THE RIGHT WINDOW OF OPPORTUNITY.

I knew that entry hadn't been there the day before. I had taken to reading The Diary every day; it brought me closer to Lizzie and my goal—OUR goal—the removal of the parents and anyone who might try to do me any further damage. I suddenly recalled a phrase Shannon had taught me when we studied the Holocaust "Those who forget the past are condemned to relive it." The parents certainly didn't know about the past I was avenging, and they were now condemned.

As I thumbed back through The Diary, I felt compelled to pause at Lizzie's description of her lover; "The musician has ebony skin that is a dazzling breath of midnight in the noonday sun, his music speaks to me. As his fingers dance across the keys, the notes waltz into my heart. His eyes locked with mine and I felt him reading the loneliness and pain my soul possesses, soothing my battle scars with each resonant chord." I immediately envisioned Doc at the piano, playing his up tempo version of Chopsticks. Could this be more than coincidence? Was it possible that two lost souls had searched each other out? I needed to find out more about Lt. Zach Murdock. I owed it to myself, and to Grandma Lizzie, she wanted to know.

CHAPTER SEVEN
~Doc~

There are plenty of 'unsolved' cases in police files, more than we care to talk about. With the lack of viable evidence at the Lex Mungo murder scene, (there was plenty of blood—all Mungo's) no fingerprints, bodily fluids other than the blood, no hair or skin samples, only the ancient, office manager of the motel mentioning seeing some woman come out to get a paper—with no worthwhile description beyond "good figure…" from the half blind clerk, Mungo was on his way to the cold case file. At the archives there that now made 2 of my cases, unsolved, which was two too many for me. There was some connection to the Morse family—Lex Mungo and Shannon Toluene a year prior. The Morse family was the only matching thread and it was a tenuous tie, but it was there. There were also the verses left at the scenes, these had not been made public—they were our bait—if any of the usual suspects—the 'I did it—arrest me' chronic confession junkies mentioned them we would know we had a live one, but so far not one of our standard flock of stool pigeons had mentioned them. So, after another 18 months of investigation, both cases went to the vaults, but mentally the cases were linked in the back of my mind, I kept digging because of the feeling I had that The Morse guardians were more than they chose to present and I didn't want to see Elizabeth hurt anymore than she had been. I kept exploring her guardian's pasts, and came up with some very provocative information. Before they had 'adopted' Elizabeth, they had taken under their joint wing another young child — this girl was about 5 when the couple — at that time Rodney and Rita Sandbern were their names — the same as the girl they were grooming — little Susanna Sandbern had a mother who wanted more than anything to see her little darling on the stage in New York. Rodney and Rita had not had a great deal of success with their own careers, but thought they could make some money with Susanna, who was said to be a talented kid. They got Susanna a decent part in a Broadway show that ran 2 years before little Susanna outgrew the role. Somehow, with no new role in the offing cute little Susanna Sandbern next showed up in a raunchy X rated version of the Shirley Temple SUSANNA OF THE MOUNTIES re-titled SUSANNA DOES THE MOUNTIES. From there little Susanna went on to be a big name in the kiddie porn business, her real mother had a nasty accident in a N.Y. alley and little Susanna eventually ended up on the N.Y streets, once her cute appeal was used up. I tried to track her down, but she had disappeared like a rat under the streets of the city that never sleeps.

 I made sure to casually drop Susanna's name the next time I stopped by the Morse home, ostensibly to say the Mungo case was in the cold case files, but I wanted them to know I knew about their past. Just hearing her name froze the pair like popsicles. I simply mentioned I wanted to know what Elizabeth's jobs were as they came up — I wanted to check and make sure they were on the up and up, you just couldn't trust some people in this business and I would make it my personal task to check up on anyone who was interested in Elizabeth for ANYTHING. Of course they made a great show of thanking me on Elizabeth's behalf, but I could smell the smoke—Mr. Morse had the thinking wheel running so fast in his head. His wife just stood, pale and shaking, not looking me in the eyes. I was pretty damn sure Elizabeth would be alright, but I would check in periodically.

CHAPTER EIGHT
~Elizabeth~

I'm not sure how he managed it, but Doc seemed to have frightened the parents with something. I had so much more freedom wasn't called upon to join into their nasty escapades and they more or less stayed out of my life. Doc became a regular fixture; I could bounce ideas off of him and be certain of an honest response. He was stopping by several times a week to see how I was getting along, what film work I was doing and taking up my free time with trips around Hollywood and the outlying areas—he even took me on a ski trip to Big Bear and taught me to ski—which became such a passion with me that I was talking him into excursions whenever I could, the parents couldn't complain—he was a police detective, I couldn't be safer. We were on a first name basis before I even realized it—he was just Zach or Doc and it was unbelievably comfortable. Zach took me through what could have been awkward teen years and into my young lady stage, he was always a gentleman and I actually wanted to tell him about my plans for the parents, explain that it was necessary for them to die the same way Andrew Borden and his evil cow of a wife had. It had to be done, then; perhaps Zach and I would go off somewhere together and start a new life. We were meant to be together, I could feel it, just as great, great grandma Lizzie had known when she met the musician in London that they were fated to be together. But then, when I was 17, fate stepped in again with an offer I didn't want to refuse—a modeling agent from the Wilhemina Agency had been watching me over the last year and liked what she saw, the agency wanted to send me to Paris for some test shots and possible print work. Paris! I wanted more than anything to go and of course talked it over with Doc. The parent's permission was of secondary concern to me—I knew that if Zach okayed it, I could be on my way; he seemed to have that much power over the parents. Zach, of course had to check out the modeling agency—but Wilhelmina is known all over the world and I knew they were on the up and up. The parents had a long discussion with Zach and decided (grudgingly) that I could pursue this new avenue. I would be on my way to Paris in 2 weeks! I packed my things; made certain my passport was in order and dreamed of the tower Eiffel as a backdrop for a new beginning, a life free of the parent's abuse, a life of my own!

Two days before my departure the parents had a sudden change of heart, they suddenly didn't feel comfortable about my heading off to Paris, without a chaperon, they felt they should accompany me. The father candidly mentioned, with a gleam in his eyes I hadn't seen for the past couple of years that the French were much more open about sexuality, and it might be worth exploring other avenues. Of course I saw right through his thinly veiled threat—he planned on taking up where Zach had more or less forced him to leave off, feeling that his peccadillo's would be overlooked in France. I was horrified; I would not go back down that path. The parents kept watch over the phone like FBI agents, not allowing me to let Zach in on their change of plans. I stormed into my room and locked myself in, after a while I picked up The Diary and read another new entry—I hadn't seen a new one since Zach became a part of my life. This one repeated the phrase: THOSE WHO FORGET THE PAST ARE CONDEMNED TO RELIVE IT! Then; YOU KNOW WHAT YOU MUST DO! THEY LEAVE YOU NO CHOICE—SHOW ANY MERCY—THEY NEVER HAVE!

I thought about it. It was so very true—the parents knew what had happened to the Borden's—they had this diary in the house, they MUST have read it, must know the story of my great, great grandmother! And I felt, they must have wanted me to know it, learn my heritage—why else have The Diary lying about, in plain sight? Again, I knew destiny was calling, and I knew the time of death was upon them. I re-read the facts of the Borden murders—I had researched the case thoroughly on the internet, this must mimic it as closely as possible—the mother first—in the guest room, followed by the father—on a chaise (which we had) in the study. I didn't have a great deal of time to plan—my flight was scheduled for day after tomorrow, so tomorrow was the day. A state of calm overtook me, I could feel Lizzie at my side, guiding my steps as I went to the tool shed and found the axe, carefully taking it upstairs while wearing my latex gloves, checking the guest room, setting the scene, so to speak—pulling down the bedcovers a bit, moving the pillows aside as if readying it for a visitor. The parents didn't question where I wandered, what I did – as long as I steered clear of the phone.

That night was what I was thinking of as The Last Supper. I sat in the center seat at the dining table, the parents on either side of me, chatting easily, feeling almost like a jungle researcher, so detached—studying wild apes, noticing for the first time how Neanderthal they were, how below my intelligence level. I thought about how I should offer them a choice as this WAS their last meal...well, maybe breakfast would be, depending on their behavior tonight. I felt so empowered—my life was my own, my fate in my hands (as was that of the parents). The parents announced that they were going out for 'one last fling' with their friends before we headed off to Paris. My stomach twisted and turned at the thought of them tagging along with me, hoping to cash in on my life a bit more. Having finished with the falsely familial bow to the American evening meal, I semi-politely refused their invitation to join them and adjourned to my room, locked the door and practiced my axe swings, I knew the childish rhyme count was off—it had not been 40 or 42 whacks, it had taken much less, but I considered going along with the rhyme just for the show. When I heard the parents finally leave and knew the telephone was unguarded, I phoned Zach and begged him to drive me to the airport in the morning. He asked if the parents wouldn't like to take me and I explained that "They had gone out partying, no doubt a sort of good riddance to bad rubbish fling celebrating my exit from their lives, and would probably oversleep in the morning, they usually did after parties and I really did not want to miss my flight,. "Besides," I told him, "I want some private time with you before I leave." Doc agreed to pick me up around 8:30 the next morning for my 10:30 flight.

I think Lizzie's spirit was in high form and eager for the action to be completed. I was pacing and between my practice swings, humming the silly rhyme and giggling—or rather Lizzie was giggling—it was a deadly serious business for me. Elizabeth knew what was at stake, Lizzie had nothing to lose—I had my entire life waiting, and was very much looking forward to it! But then I thought, "So is she..."

That night the parents had an early demise. Around 1 a.m. there was a rattling of my door knob and the father asked to come in—"for old times sake, sweetheart" I sat up in my bed, my anger boiling, I felt my eyes boring a hole in that rattling doorknob—I felt as though I was Eleanor Vance in THE HAUNTING—the old black and white film version of Shirley Jackson's book that had scared me no end, my right hand instinctively gripping the axe, I waited to see if the door would begin to bulge inward, forcing me to fly at it, axe flying. But I held back, even when he said "Come on, open up baby, mommy and I want to show you something, we learned a new trick at the party."

Then the mothers wheedling voice, "Yes, open up baby girl—Daddy needs some fun. Come and play"

I sat in a stony silence, chanting to myself," Tomorrow, tomorrow, tomorrow "and gripping the axe, listening. They finally gave up and went away—to amuse each other, I imagine. I left them to it and attempted to sleep, but it was hopeless now—I was constantly hearing footsteps and rattling, waiting for another unwanted overture. I was a wreck by 4 a.m. when the noise and awful laughter and moaning interspersed with screams finally died down...I set down the axe I had clutched all night and picked up The Diary, flipping to the final new entry—'DO IT, DO IT, AND DO IT NOW!!!" I closed the diary, stripped bare and headed to the guest room, where I was sure the parent's raunchy show had transpired, it usually did—the father disappearing to the study, once appeased.

The mother was sleeping, peacefully spent, on the bed, not quite the correct position, but "Oh well" I thought as I brought the axe up and let it crash into her skull. Once, twice, three times. The mother's lifeless body slumped to the floor as I pulled out the axe, staring at brains and skull adorning the headboard. Not a sound had escaped her. Perfect. "MORE" I felt Lizzie insist, and I added 37 more whacks to the body attached to the crumpled skull, leaving her awash in her own blood and I pretty well saturated too. I viewed the scene with a director's eye—Lex would have been impressed I thought, entering the guest bathroom and cleaning myself off, putting on a pair of the mother's slippers before proceeding, still naked, downstairs to the study.

I saw him, lying on the chaise, as if he was waiting, expecting me. I heard a noise, it was me—I wanted him to wake. He sat up groggy with sleep, perhaps thinking he was dreaming, "You're beautiful" he said, he must have thought it was a dream.

I raised the axe and replied, "You are NOT coming to Paris! They phoned—the country is closed to perverts!" bringing it down into his slightly balding pate, again and again, Lizzie held the axe, but it was years of abuse at the father's hands that powered my swings. I struck until he was unrecognizable. Whacked at him until my energy was spent, my pent up well of hurt and anger finally dry. Then I did the finishing touch—placed the bloody carcass so its feet were neatly off of the floor. I proceeded back up to my room, the bloodied slippers leaving marks on the carpet—but foot marks much larger than mine. I never looked back, not curious at all as to what was left behind. That was the past—Paris was the future and I needed to be sure everything was packed and ready to leave this sorry excuse for a life.

I felt an enormous wave of relief wash over me as I re-entered my room, having taken the blood soaked slippers off at the top of the stairs. I went immediately into my bathroom and turned on the shower, stepped in and cleaned off all remnants of the chaos that had just taken place. I scrubbed with my loofah and my SERENITY body wash, when I was totally cleansed, I sank onto the floor of the shower, wrapped my arms around my naked body and cried. I wasn't sure what I was crying about—certainly not the loss of my tormentors. I think maybe I was crying about the loss of the woman I would have been, had I grown up in a life without the abuse I had been taught to believe was a normal way of life. All I know is, I sat and cried in the showers unending rain until I was cried out. I turned off the shower, dried myself with a fresh towel and went out and curled up on my bed with The Diary. I fell into a calm sleep after reading the new entry—WE'RE FREE.

I awoke about 2 hours later, famished I threw on my robe and padded down to the kitchen through the silent house. I bypassed the den, no reason, I just took the longer route to the kitchen and began tossing anything loose into a frying pan with three beaten eggs as the base—leftover chicken I tore into shreds, the remnants of a red bell pepper quickly diced along with it's yellow cousin, a small dollop of salsa, some crumbled bacon—everything I could grab went into the monster omelet, which I topped off with shredded Monterey jack cheese. I set my place neatly at the kitchen table, sat in the blessed silence and ate like I had never eaten before. My stomach wasn't in knots and I felt free to eat my fill. I devoured about three quarters of the gigantic breakfast, cleaned up the table and phoned Zach to remind him of the 8:30 pick up time and tell him that "yes, the parents were out until the wee hours and were now dead asleep" I think Lizzie made me say that, Zach would have appreciated the dark humor if I could tell him—he was a very special person to me—and to Lizzie.

"It's fine with my guardians, they're relieved they don't have to get up, just want me to phone when I arrive in Paris"" I explained to him when he asked if I was certain they wouldn't want to take me and I assured him "they won't care one way or the other Zach, and I do want some time to say goodbye to you without them around." That comment seemed to put him at ease and he agreed to come by at about 8:30. Paris, here I come!

I gathered everything, without going anywhere near the guest room or den, and had my bags at the front door, my passport in my purse and a gift I had for Zach—to remember me by in my absence. I had found a beautiful ruby and onyx ring for him—he had let slip that his birthday was in July so I had checked to see what his birthstone was, Ruby—so perfect! I had it set with an onyx because Lizzie had mentioned her lover wearing an onyx ring—"as black as his midnight eyes"

I saw his car pull up promptly at 8:00 and slipped out the door as if being careful not to awaken the sleeping parents, and ran to his car, jumped in after tossing my bags into the back and kissed him with an ardor even I didn't expect. I blushed and apologized, saying, "Oh, I guess I'm a little excited to be going to Paris!" I was embarrassed, but it was an emotional move, not something meant to convey anything, or so I thought.

CHAPTER NINE
~Zach~

I picked the girl up at eight, for her 10:30 am flight to Paris, we had plenty of time, the journey from her house would only take about twenty minutes, and as I eased the car onto the freeway amid the vague early chatter about weather and what airlines were good to fly on, I wondered why I had agreed to take her; was it just that I had a protective feel towards this young waif, due to the abysmal start I knew she'd had in her short life, or was it more than that? Did I feel some kind of kinship or attachment to her, or even more was I attracted to her? And if it was that, how did I feel about it?

She was of course, much younger that I, and to that extent, should I ever decide to take things further, I knew I would come under all kinds of criticism, or at least reflection, not least from Chance, who would no doubt have an opinion, and regard any relationship as he usually did, with the same kind of calculation he used for all things in life; was the gamble worth the possible return; and somehow, despite my misgivings, I was beginning to think it would be.

She was full of chatter about her first trip abroad, and to the very romantic city of Paris, and especially enthusiastic about being away from the parents, whom she told me had finally relented, with a little pressure from me, and had actually managed to rouse themselves, been up and wished her a good trip as she had left the house.

I didn't tell her that while she was away, I would be doing some further investigation into the parents and their so called care, as I felt that they had taken her in for one reason and one reason only, their own satisfaction, and maybe a little profit on the side, little did I know then, as we drove, just how true that would turn out to be. As I aimed at the LAX turnoff, her casual question slid into my thought pattern…

"So detective, what will you be busy with, while I'm away, are you still working on the two murders, or have you moved on to something more interesting? "

"Oh there are not too many things more interesting than murder" I said to her, as I looked for the parking signs for her terminal, and slid my car into a short term bay.
"I have enough to keep me busy while you're gone, and I'll try not to miss you too much, and keep myself busy with making life difficult for your guardians."

She had glanced across at me with a half smile, looking pleased with herself, when I had mentioned that I might miss her, and kept quiet, as if in thought as I found a porter for her bags, and walked with her to the AA check-in desk. After the formalities of check in, we went to the departure gate, and with her first class ticket, she could go into the comfort of a decent and semi private lounge to wait for her flight to be called; we stood at the entrance a little awkwardly, something hanging there between us, until I smiled and said to her :

"Well, here you are—all ready for your first adventure, take care of yourself, and let me know if you need collecting when you get back…"

She gave a small sigh, as if in recognition of temporary parting, and warmed my day with a broad beaming smile…"Oh, I will Zach," she said…"And you make sure you take care of yourself while I'm gone, don't get into any scrapes that you can't handle…" Laughing, I put my hand on her shoulder…

"I won't, and if I do, I have a friend arriving who'll make sure I get out in one piece, he's a buddy from way back, an English guy, a gambler, but the most reliable person I've ever met, so I'll be quite safe while you're gone, and maybe we can all get together for dinner when you're back…?"

She looked thoughtful for a moment, then her face broke into another smile, and she gave me the reply I needed…

"I'd like that…" she said, "and it will be good to meet your friend, and ask him some questions about you, got to get to know your secrets somehow, I'll look forward to it, and I'll look forward to seeing you too…" she reached into her purse and dug out a small box, and whispered "Happy birthday Zach" turning a rosier shade of café au lait. With that she stepped forward and put her arms around me, reaching up and brushing her lips across mine, it felt like being brushed by fire wrapped in glass, like the whispered touch of something ethereal, either an angel, or a ghost, and then she turned and was gone.

Walking back out to my car, I began to wonder just what I was getting into, briefly—she was a suspect, only because of her association with both victims, but that wasn't really why I had doubts, was it the age difference? No, there was just something I couldn't quite put my finger on; oh well, I'd let it go for now, and spend the time she was away trying to come up with some leads on the two cases, maybe they weren't even related, right now, I just wasn't sure, but I knew one thing, I was looking forward to seeing Chance, and getting his perspective, both on the cases, and also my feelings for the girl; and I could just see him now, his eyebrows raising, and hear him as he tossed out one of his epithets. 'Oh no, Zach's gone and bought a ticket again, watch out world, now we're all in trouble…' Maybe he'd be right, maybe we would be, but somehow, like him, I knew I'd still have to buy the ticket, and follow the game until we all knew what the prize was. I opened the small box and with a smile placed Elizabeth's gift on my right hand ring finger. Was I making a promise? To her, a promise to myself? I wasn't certain, but I was anxious to find out.

CHAPTER TEN
~Elizabeth~

I didn't think about it again, I just reached up and kissed Zach, it seemed the thing to do, then I dashed down the causeway and went through all the security procedures with my head in the clouds and probably a silly grin on my face. I found my way to the VIP lounge where the representative from Wilhelmina was to meet me, and found him easily. I had met Rolf in Los Angeles at my first interview—he was a mincing little limp wristed man in a splash of fuchsia and tangerine and the attitude to carry it off—waiting with two other young hopefuls who would also be going to Paris; Jordache and Keisha. As we introduced ourselves, I began to wonder if my fairly common name—Elizabeth would stay with me or I would be re-christened something more exotic.

As we boarded the flight I knew I was in for it when the in-flight movie was announced; RUNAWAY was one of my well known feature films. The one Zach had shown the parents a photo from with me on Lex Mungo's arm at the premiere. As the film started, Jordache and Keisha acted like old time buddies as every other passenger seemed to wander by on the way to the restroom or to ask a flight attendant a question. I semi-graciously signed drink napkins for the two children sitting behind us and a not so timid grandmotherly type, "Just write To My dear friend Ada" she suggested after patting me on the cheek.

    Hoping to keep a low profile for the rest of the flight, I donned my headphones and closed my eyes, visions of Zach dancing through my mind. I realized I could still feel the tingle I had had when I kissed him. I had never really kissed a man before—I refused to kiss any of the actors or friends the parents forced me to copulate with on film—and that was what it was, copulation. I wouldn't even grace it with the word sex—it was a forced action that I lived through by going on auto pilot and travelling mentally to my white room, and it certainly had nothing to do with LOVE. I relived the jolt I had felt when I kissed Zach, sending flutters to my stomach, my heart, maybe even deep in my soul. Was this what Lizzie had felt with her musician? If it was—I wanted another dose of it. Zach had never made a move on me—he had always acted more like an older brother, but I thought, "He's not THAT much older than me...nothing like those old perverts and paid sex machines I had been forced to endure. Zach was young and vital, handsome and thoughtful. Could I be falling in love with Zach Murdock? This could complicate things, but that didn't halt the kaleidoscope of images that swirled in my head; Zach teaching me to ski, sitting at the grand piano playing his up tempo version of Chopsticks, and the time he had taken me to a Chinese Restaurant in honour of 'our song' and the fun I had had trying the interesting new foods; Dim Sum with it's great things like shredded chicken fun rolls and barbequed pork buns. I smiled my way to Paris listening to the canned muzak.

When we finally landed at Charles deGalle International airport, I was in a strange state of euphoria, maybe the result of the jet lag I had been warned about or perhaps all the thoughts about Zach Murdock I had entertained myself with.

Jordache, Keisha and I would be sharing a stunning suite at our ultra modern hotel. We tossed our bags in our rooms and made a beeline to the phone to call our respective guardians. Keisha and Jordache got right through and chattered away, I got an unending ring. I finally hung up and phoned Zach, knowing that with the time difference he would likely be 'detecting', but I wanted to at least hear his voice. After two rings I heard:"Hey this is Zach Murdock—leave all the pertinent info and I'll catch up with you!" I smiled at his friendly tone and said—"It's Elizabeth, I'm in Paris, in one piece and ready for the city of lights. Talk to you soon, Detective" and hung up the phone as Jordache and Keisha looked on with a very interested air. I shrugged, smiled at them and simply said, "My parole officer." We all laughed and agreed jet lag or not we HAD to go to the Eiffel Tower, which we could see from the window in our sitting room.

That week was a whirlwind of activity—photo shoots, publicity and as much sightseeing as we could fit in, which was not easy. I think I was considering this a holiday of sorts, but Rolf thought differently—he rushed us from one event to another, interspersing photo shoots and paparazzi gatherings. Being used to the hurry up and wait involved with the motion picture business, this was a totally new animal to me. I phoned the house every night, always getting the endless ringing and wondering when I would hear from Zach. I drifted off to sleep with him in my dreams every night and so wanted to see him, touch him again. I had never felt this way before; it was intoxicating-wondrous highs followed by devastating lows. I felt Zach's lips on mine, imagined what it would be like to have him hold me close, and literally ached for him.

It took 8 days for the call to come. It was 8:00 p.m. Paris time, we had just returned from a 'short day' when I picked up the phone and heard Zach's voice say; "your guardians are dead." It was a shock to actually hear the words, combined with the impact of actually hearing Zach's voice the realization of what he was saying took a moment to register, "Elizabeth? Are you still with me?" he asked.

It was as if I was on another planet instead of a different continent—Zach's voice buzzing in my head along with the humming of the sing song rhyme, 'Lizzie Borden took an axe...' and the worried faces of Jordache and Keisha looking at me with concern. Suddenly, the room was spinning and the lights were out. I vaguely felt the telephone receiver sliding from my hand as my body turned to jelly and slid away from reality itself.

CHAPTER ELEVEN
~Zach~

I drove by Elizabeth's house quite a few times, telling myself I was just keeping my word to make her guardians nervous (I never saw them at all, so I guessed it was working) but knowing that somehow I just wanted to stay connected with her. I was missing the little jaunts I would take her on, missing the look of cautious wonder at the new things I would introduce her to, untried foods, new sports (my God! The girl didn't know how to ski, had never even been in the snow!) These things were such a treat for her they became new to me again. I felt like a kid again, back on the streets of London, playing hooky from my classes at RADA. I argued back and forth with myself on the age difference—on one hand telling myself I was too old to even consider a relationship with the girl, on the other reasoning that she would be 18 in a few weeks and I wasn't that much older than her, she was mature in a lot of ways and still a kid in a few—that was part of what attracted me I suppose—Elizabeth's amazement at things that had become so commonplace to me. I wanted to show her things she had never seen, and see things commonplace to me, now new and shining for the first time with her so that we could share the fascination, the awe there was to behold in the world—shit—I just wanted to be with her again. I would gaze at the ring she had given me as though it was a piece of her wrapped around my finger.

I needed someone to talk this through with. There really wasn't anyone at the station I could confide in, they were associates, not really friends I would feel comfortable discussing my 'could be love life' with. Not something I would want to share with my folks—yet. Chance kept popping into my head. I had mentioned him to Elizabeth, maybe it was time to talk to him in person again, and it had been a few years. I decided it was time to buy Chance a ticket into this game.

I had finally made the decision and was driving past Elizabeth's house again on Wednesday morning when I saw the gardener come barrelling out of the front door. I knew Manuel came by once a month to take care of the yard and the plants indoors—they had several impressive bromeliads he kept looking healthy and beautiful. Right now, however, Manuel was looking far from healthy himself. He was, in fact vomiting into the flower beds in front of the house. I pulled to the curb and jumped out of my car. Manuel knew me from my many visits while Elizabeth was still in the states and wiped his mouth on the bandana from his pocket and began poring forth a tale of mayhem in the house, so fast I could barely understand him. I stepped into my detective persona and called the station for back up before entering.

I smelled it before I even walked in—death hung over the house like a black cloud. For a moment all I could think was 'thank God Elizabeth's in Paris', knowing something unsavoury was waiting inside. I found the father first—or what I assumed was the father. The putrid body was lying on the sofa in the den, hacked up like a novice butcher had taken a first exam on its head. It was bare naked and probably would have been quite comfortable if alive and breathing. I covered my mouth and nose with a handkerchief and looked around some more, careful not to touch anything before the crime scene team got here—because it obviously WAS the scene of a crime. Again I thanked all that is holy that Elizabeth was not here and continued up the stairs. I carefully stepped over a pair of bloody slippers at the top of the stairs and peeked into the rooms off the hallway. I found the mothers body in a bedroom two doors down, in pretty much the same condition as the father's had been. I heard the siren's announcing the CSI team's arrival, and headed back downstairs to let them in to do what they do best. I would jump in when they had done the initial once and twice over—I was determined to find out what had happened here—and to be the one to let Elizabeth know what had happened.

I was brought into the case officially when the CSI team found the poem in Elizabeth's room. It was tossed on her bed like an afterthought by whoever had perpetrated the crime.

Unrecognizable demons, now crushed to a pulp
No more haunting children's dreams
No longer forcing that unwelcome gulp
You found your way here, I wonder how?
Demons sent back to hell, your original home
Leaving the innocent free to roam
Leaving the innocent free to roam
Leaving the innocent free—for now…

It ended there, tying the killer to the other two cases and chilling my heart with the thought that Elizabeth might be next on this madman's 'to do list'. Were they all tied to Elizabeth? Did someone have a twisted vendetta against the girl who had become so entrenched in my soul?

But what was the key, there had to be something that linked them all, my best guess was that it was something to do with family, but of course, 'the parents' were not related to her by blood, and neither were the first two victims (to my knowledge), so what was the common denominator, what was it that tied the victims of all these killings to my Elizabeth?

Somewhere, in her short past, was where I would find the answer, and perhaps in the reasons that she was put up for adoption, maybe the missing piece of the puzzle lay with her birth mother, or some deep dark family secret, perhaps somewhere in the past, there was a family black sheep that I didn't know about, but I was certainly going to find out, and perhaps for the search I could use some help, and also a little brotherhood, it was time I thought to call Chance, and get his perspective on this little mystery.

CHAPTER TWELVE
~Elizabeth~

I went from a whirlwind of activity in Paris to a whirlpool of strange voices and frightening thoughts sloshing through shades of grey and violet with bright splashes of dark red in my brain as I sat aboard an airliner headed back to L.A. It was a total blur from the moment I had heard Zach's voice on the phone—fainting away (I was told), Keisha tossing water on my face, Jordache having run to get Rolf, who was totally useless outside of his sphere of organizing modelling shoots and press meetings, the hotel manager arranging a flight home per Zach's directions with the assurance that Monsieur Murdock would be waiting for me at the airport. I don't remember the flight home, although I know they didn't play a film I was featured in—no one bothered me for an autograph. I stood, impatiently in the immigration line, praying that Zach would be at the desk when I was cleared.

He was and I greeted him the same way I had said

goodbye, only this time Zach returned my kiss, just as I had dreamed he would. We didn't speak; I simply clung to him, silently sobbing, never wanting to release my hold—I wanted this moment to last forever. Finally I relaxed my death grip and just looked up at him, and that one look told me everything would work out, and I had noticed with pleasure that he was wearing the ring I had given him when I departed for Paris, telling me indeed, it would all be alright, but Lizzie's voice hummed in the background—"not if you tell, not if you tell…" making my sobs even louder. I wanted this to work but I couldn't start a relationship, a real relationship, for the first time in my life, with lies. Zach held me and let me cry in his arms until the waterworks dried up, then we retrieved my bags and headed to the parking lot. Once we got in his car we both just sat until I said, "Please don't take me back to that house". He fired up the car and drove out of the parking garage with great determination.

CHAPTER THIRTEEN
~Zach~

I couldn't take her back to the house—it was a crime scene—entry blocked off with the recognizable bright yellow tape. And I realised I didn't want to take her anywhere but to my apartment. As I had held her shaking, sobbing body close I knew I was going to step out of the lines, and I didn't care. I just wanted Elizabeth to be safe and I knew I could give her that feeling of safety—I wanted her to be comforted by me—not some unknown social worker. I knew at least a little of what made her tick, and I wanted, God help me to know everything that made her this intoxicating young woman. And I wanted her to know me—know Zachary Austin Murdock and all my demons—and loving her was definitely one of those demons. Elizabeth had somehow worked her way under my skin and into what I had thought was an impenetrable fortress—my heart. I tore out of the garage like Satan himself was after me—and maybe he was, Elizabeth was an under age female (at least by 6 weeks) and an almost material witness to a crime that I was investigating, having lived in the house of the victims, but I didn't care. For that instant in time I wasn't a cop—I was a man. We didn't speak on the drive; she just sat with her hand lightly on my hand, which rested on the stick shift. When we got to my place she just looked at me and said "I don't even know how to drive a stick shift."

I just put my hand over hers, which was still resting on mine on the stick shift and replied, "I'll teach you," and she leaned over and kissed me again. I couldn't stop myself, I didn't want to stop myself, I returned her kiss with a fervour I hadn't felt since…well since kissing her this morning. I broke it, finally, and we got out of the car. Elizabeth stood watching me get her bags out of the car and followed me up the 3 steps to the door of my Spanish style ground floor apartment. I dropped her bags on the floor inside the door saying awkwardly. "Are you hungry?"

Elizabeth just looked at me for a moment then melted into my arms again, "Just hold me." she requested. I did, inhaling her fragrance, a kind of cinnamon scent mixed with unrecognised floral, then I bent and kissed her head, she lifted her face and we were wrapped in each other again. I'm not sure how we ended up in my bedroom, but we did. It was a soft, slow trip to the clouds—I didn't want to stop it—I don't think I could have, I wanted her that much. It was as if we were part of some unwritten love song and I wanted it to play on forever. I was totally enveloped in her smell, her taste, and the soft sounds she made. I knew I was breaking the law, but somehow, for the first time, I didn't care.

CHAPTER FOURTEEN
~Chance~

My name is Richard Chance, Chance by name and chance by nature, my old Grandma always used to say, and I guess she was right.

When I was a kid, I was always the one to climb the big tree, jump off the high wall, or pick the big guy's door for "knockdown ginger."

It just grew from there, and became a kind of life philosophy for me; if there was something on offer, any kind of chance of excitement, profit, or just an interesting encounter, then I'd take it, and, even though chances nearly always have consequences, just like actions have reactions, that never bothered me, well rarely anyway.

This liking for chance manifested itself mostly, in my work, I am a professional gambler, Horses sometimes, greyhounds for recreation, but for work, mostly cards, and then mostly poker.

GAME OF CHANCE

I play all kinds of poker, and there are many, but mostly a game known as "Texas Holdem ," sometimes tournaments, even on television, you may just know my face, if you watch the cable channels in the early hours, but mostly cash games. Games where you sit down with your stake, and get up broke, or rich with everyone else's money, but whatever, you don't get up until it's over.

Chance enters my private life to, I always seem to pick either friends, or even lovers, who end up giving me their all, or costing me my own; but that is just me, never cautious, always all or nothing, too often for my liking lately, it's been nothing.

As my favorite singer, Garth Brooks, says, 'I coulda missed the pain, but I'da had to miss the dance', or in other words, if you never buy a ticket, you'll never win a prize.

My problem is, sometimes I buy a ticket when I don't even know what the prize is, even when I win it, and sometimes, even when I know what it is, and I don't want it, I still buy the ticket.

Yes, that's my problem alright, I just can't, not take part, whatever the venue, whoever's dealing, whatever the odds, I just can't stay out of the game; cards or life.

When I first saw Doc, I almost missed him, he was hunched over in his chair staring intently at his cards, playing blackjack…a fools game, unless it's just for recreation, and you have a mind like a computer; he wasn't stand out in stature, smooth good looks like a young Sidney Poitier, but he didn't really give off an aura, until later.

I don't really like casinos, not for serious play…I was here to leave someone a message, and felt like throwing some money away; in these places, even before you play, you've lost, and even if you win, a percentage of your 'luck, goes to the house;

Gambling for me is about people, not businesses, one to one, take his money, or he takes yours; but, tonight was just for fun, so I was prepared to lose a few hundred at Baccarat, and of course the cards ran for me. Then I tossed a few chips at the Roulette table, the game you'll never win, and did; and after a quiet celebratory drink, walked out of the hall with around three grand of their money, except of course, it's not theirs, it's some strangers, but whatever, never look a gift horse and all that.

As I walked through the underground car-park to the sovereign, they came out from between parked cars, two in front, two behind that I couldn't see, but could feel.
Normally, I would have just thrown them the money, it really wasn't much, and I wasn't in the mood to fight a losing battle, but they just had a look that annoyed me,
A smugness that said they'd already won; so I said nothing, simply kicked the first one hard, under the left knee, and waited to be engulfed.

I expected the two behind to jump me, but all I heard was the sound of quiet thudding, and it never happened, and before I could take the third one, a figure came past me, athletic, almost ballet like, and the last one went down, hard.
Then he turned to me, and I saw Doc smile, and that was when I knew we'd become friends, he had a smile that lit up a room, and the violence that had erupted, vanished just as quickly, as he said., "You want to call the law, or get a drink…?"
We went to breakfast at my favourite haunt, the Dorchester, and over a few Mimosa's and large plates of various dead animals, he told me that he had been here studying at RADA, and struggling to become an actor, but wasn't sure it was really what he wanted; he had some crazy idea that he wanted to be a 'gentleman' gambler, like the old riverboat days, so, as a small thank you, I took him with me, the next day, to a friendly game, well, when I say friendly, the sit down was only a grand, so that was all you could lose, and lose he did, quickly, and far too easily; as it happens I lost too, although it took longer, and in

the end, I gave it away, he was distracting me too much.

We knocked around together for a few days, I showed him my London, not the tourist spots, but the real London, the people, the places where real life occurs; and when it came time, the following Sunday, for him to fly home to the States for a family thing, we parted at the airport, with me giving him some advice that somehow he never regretted.

"Forget gambling..." I said to him, "You're crap at it, you want to win too much, and that's not what it's about. You want to make a living, not live for the buzz, and when you need to win, you won't, give it up, before you become hooked and it destroys you."

And then I said, almost as a joke..."Go do something your analytical mind can cope with, be a detective or something, somewhere you can use your meagre acting talent in some way that'll have results..."

I didn't know at the time he'd take me so literally, and didn't know then, that Zach Murdock and I would become real friends, not just acquaintances, the kind of friends who even if we didn't see each other all that often, would slip into that easy familiarity in the way only real friends can when they meet.

Over the next five years, we met only a handful of times, sometimes in London, sometimes in the US, twice on foreign soil; on holidays we arranged by mutual agreement, but always, always it was easy, and comfortable.

Whenever we talked, either by telephone, or messenger, he asked after my luck, and, good or bad, never once criticised my lifestyle, and I followed his lightening rise in the police department with a slightly detached amusement; me, with a copper as a friend, what would my nefarious variety of so called friends have said, but it never mattered to me, the man was my friend.

CHAPTER FIFTEEN
~Elizabeth~

It was amazing. My Life, which had always seemed to be wrapped up in celluloid was now an old black and white tear jerker romance-in short, it was suddenly almost perfect. Zach made me feel so—human. When I was making love with Zach—we were making love. It wasn't some tawdry scripted camera ready imitation—it was more real than anything had ever been for me. I wasn't being evaluated, primped for camera readiness, I was being loved. I was being reborn into a creature who had done no wrong, everything had been erased, the slate wiped clean. There was a bizarre, surreal moment when Zach murmured "Lizzie..." into my ear and then Lizzie interrupted my thoughts with brief comments— letting me know this is how it had been for her and...the thought ended as I was swept again into everything that was Zach. I was, at last, being LOVED, and not used.

I'm not certain just how long it lasted? Forever? A moment

in time that would always be a part of me...I do recall falling asleep in his arms, to be awakened later and continuing the glorious exploration of forever—"If this is what death is—take me now" I recall thinking, "eternal bliss" repeated my soul, pushing away other less pleasant memories which followed the thought that I would HAVE to tell Zach the truth. "Tomorrow..." I said in an imitation of Scarlett O'Hara, "I'll think about it tomorrow."

CHAPTER SIXTEEN
~Zach~

    I'm not sure when I decided that THIS time it was worth it to play against the rules, colour outside of the lines. I don't know what exactly it was about her—the vulnerability mixed with her toughness, the ability to keep fighting against what should have seemed like insurmountable odds (if my suspicions were correct). Ellie was a fighter, must have always been a fighter. She was a rock—but wrapped in an amazing soft and sensuous skin—her whole persona seemed to cry out for me to hold her, protect her, and love her. I could see my entire career going down in a flaming blaze, but the flame I felt when she was in my arms, when I was one with her, shut out anything else. Elizabeth was the stuff my dreams were made of. I had never put much stock in the thought of 'soul mates'—but…Something told me to get to know everything there was to know about Elizabeth Ann Morse, an instinct maybe, but whatever it was I had no desire to argue with it.

I had been with other women, but they had never meant enough to me to risk everything for. I'm not some kind of a roving Romeo, don't get me wrong. I was fond of the women I had been with—but Ellie…Elizabeth seemed to possess me. It was the first time I had ever felt like I HAD to make love to a woman—no choice, I HAD to explore every part of her—physically, mentally AND emotionally, it was necessary to my well being. God help me—it was necessary to my sanity—I was driven…maybe Chance could help me figure out what was happening, but for now, I was going to jump into the fire.

There was something about this girl, this woman that seemed to haunt me, it had from the first time I interviewed her. She seemed almost a dual personality—maybe it came from having spent all of her life as an actress, but it seemed as if there had to be more to it. I began to wonder about siblings—she didn't know of any, but that didn't mean there might not be some, hell, she could have a twin and not know about it. That thought stuck in the back of my mind, I would ask Gail, if assigning her to the case was okayed, to pursue it—but gently.

I knew full well that Ellie could not stay here in my apartment. I let them know at the station that I had picked her up at the airport, but the thought of going to the house that was now a crime scene was too overwhelming and besides she was exhausted, so I would let her stay at my place in the extra bedroom and we would get her sorted out in the morning. The higher ups went along with it for the night—that glorious night…

In the morning I checked with my landlord—there was an empty apartment in the complex the P.D. could have for her. I got the okay to have Gail Hoyle, a very near to retirement policewoman to stay with her when needed, which wouldn't be too often I assured Gail who was enjoying light duties until she could collect her retirement checks. I made sure she knew that I would still need access to Elizabeth as she was a vital part of my case (and now, my life—although I kept that to myself)) I had Gail Hoyle assigned to watch over Ellie for several reasons; she had years of experience and a motherly nature under a rock solid police exterior. She might just pick up on something I was missing, perhaps I was getting too close to the subject, I was having rather bizarre ideas, possibilities that were probably far fetched—anything to keep Ellie in the clear, I guess.

CHAPTER SEVENTEEN
~Ellie meets Gail~

Officer Gail Hoyle was to be a sort of chaperone/watchdog for me while I stayed in a nearby apartment that Zach had arranged for through the LAPD. I found her to be a pleasant enough woman who talked incessantly about her "Dear, departed husband Hank, the love of my life—you'll know when you find yours dear, my son Ellery – we named him after the legendary detective—have you read Ellery Queen? Says I could talk a parrot to death, always saying it to his kids—my darling grandchildren—I call them the three little pigs because they gobble up everything I bake, isn't that cute? My daughter in law doesn't care for it—says it will encourage gluttony in them—isn't that a silly idea? I'm their grandma, it's my job! My daughter is still in Massachusetts—I miss Fall River—that's my home town—lived there for 60 years, just came out here when Hank passed on—too many memories there, good memories, but we all have to move on with our lives when loved ones pass, don't you think? Oh, I'm sorry dear—of course you do, but the pain is still fresh with you—it'll pass-Queenie (that's what we call my daughter—her real name is Holly—Holly Noelle Hoyle—she was a Christmas present) Ellery had moved out here and was always telling me about the glorious weather—the Golden State Ma—they don't call it that for nothin' he'd say—so I finally up and came out—Holly is in the old house—I guess there will always be a Hoyle in that house…Holly has two boys, so they may just inherit the house when I'm gone to meet up with Hank for one last hand and one last dance—we did love to dance, quite a pair we were—our friends called us Fred and Ginger Hoyle—isn't that cute? Loved to play poker too—don't tell—it's my little secret passion."

Gail can go on forever, without a pause for breath—she is amazing, although it can tire a person out trying to keep track of everything that comes pouring out. Although I didn't really think it was important to keep track of what she said, Lizzie did—I found some notes in The Diary that night—ASK MORE ABOUT FALL RIVER! So, I knew I had better find out more of Gail's home town, I knew Lizzie wanted to know, and in a way, it now seemed that Lizzie was in charge of the game—calling the shots with her diary entries pointing me in the right direction. We were a good team, Lizzie and I.

CHAPTER EIGHTEEN
~The Electric Flamingo~

The Electric Flamingo was heaving tonight, in more ways than one, the drink was flowing, the smoke was thick, and the Ribs 'n' Fries were selling thick and fast, much more than their average quality should have done, to people who were far too 'gone' to know any better, the 60's music was crashing out hard and heavy, and the smell of 60's substances hung sweetly in the atmosphere, along with the background scent of wet wood and alcohol, and the undertones of burnt meat and barbecue sauce, it made a loud statement, "don't come in here unless you're of 'the' generation."

Monday nights were usually quite quiet, but for some reason there was a crowd in, and that meant that Starshine was busy behind the bar, pouring drinks, serving what passed for food here, and keeping an eye on the transitory waitresses, making sure they didn't short change anyone, unless Starshine got her cut, and also that the customers didn't take too many liberties with the girls, although neither she nor they ever knew quite where the line was drawn.

Manfred Mann's version of 'Mighty Quinn' was blaring out of the cheap speakers, and many of the crowd were dancing, or rather swaying drunkenly, in time with the chorus that everybody knew, and Starshine herself sang along with Paul Jones…' come on without, come on within…
You've not seen nothing like the Mighty Quinn…'

Starshine poured herself another shot of mild oblivion, and began to watch the obviously out of place lady sitting at the end of the bar, watching the crowd and drinking mineral water and lime; either she was a cop (but probably not) or some kind of social worker? When they had a lull, Starshine, being naturally nosy, would ask her.
"Would you like that drink refreshed?"
"No thank you, I'll be going shortly, I only came here to kill a little time."
"Well honey, that's why most people come here, to kill time or relive it, like me. Most of us here are stuck in the past, but not you, you're a people watcher, I thought you might be a cop, or a social worker, looking for someone?"
The woman gave a small laugh…"No, I'm neither, but I am a people watcher, or rather I watch some people, actually I study people, or some people, I'm a Doctor, Lynne Uhl…"
The woman held a slim, beautifully manicured hand across the bar, and Starshine shook it, smiling…
"Sister, I'd love a job like that, just watching folk, I've had a lot of practice—does it pay?"
Lynne smiled and showed no offence at the question…

"Yes it does, but what I actually do is study twins, and especially single births that should have been twins, as well as

DNA and Chimera, I came to Fall River to check out the Lizzie Borden story, she was supposed to be a twin you know."

"Was she now —Groovy…no, I didn't know that, funny thing, this is too weird, you know? I had a kid once, a girl, and they told me, the doctors at the free clinic, that I was having twins, but there was only ever one…"

"Really, that is a coincidence, would there be any chance of speaking to her, I'd love to ask her some questions?"

"Yeah, well I'd love to too, but I gave her up for adoption when she was about 5 or 6 months old, never seen her since, although I have wondered, many times, how she's doing…"

"Oh, I'm sorry, didn't mean to bring back sad memories, just my natural inquisitiveness coming out, I can't help it."

"It's cool. Don't let it worry you sweetie, we're all nosy, and if I ever hear from her, I'll ask her if she'll talk to you to, you know…talk…"

There was a sudden rush that seemed like everyone in the bar wanted serving at one time, and Starshine was frantically busy for ten minutes without let up, when she looked up again, the woman had gone, and there on the bar, was a business card, with her name and number, and on the reverse a note, 'if you ever find your daughter, call me…' Starshine smiled ruefully,' if my daughter ever finds me, you mean…yeah fat chance', and she threw the card beneath the bar, and started on yet another round of drinks for the large group near the stage, forgetting the conversation altogether, as the booze flowed and the unmistakable voice of Bob Dylan broke into 'Just Like a Woman', yes thought Starshine, isn't it just.

The Electric Flamingo was throbbing…

CHAPTER NINETEEN
~Chance Arrives~

When I heard from him, and he asked me to come over and listen to a problem he had, I didn't hesitate; London, and it's never ending round of win and lose, was wearing on me, and so the prospect of seeing my friend, and some light entertainment was appealing; if I had known then, what I know now, I'd have done the opposite, or would I? You know me, whatever the prize; it's the ticket that I can't resist.

So I flew in, and he met me at the airport, and it began, the opening chapter, the ticket, once bought, had to be seen through, only then, as always, I didn't even know the prize, or the possible outcome, if I had, for once in my life, even I would have folded my hand.

As I walked through customs, and stood in the queue at immigration, I could see Doc standing at the desk, his face already beaming with that smile that would light up a football stadium; I told the immigration officer I was here to play poker, and take lots of money off of gullible Americans, and he had the good grace to laugh, as he stamped me for 90 days, and then I was shaking Doc's hand as he took my case and led me towards his car for the short ride into town.

We chatted briefly about each others lives, and the state of health of our respective families, and where we were going tonight; somewhere we could get a good steak, a decent bottle of claret, and then on to a game of cards, a friendly one, so that Doc couldn't lose too much, however hard he tried.

We sat in traffic and the small talk died, I asked him to tell me why he had invited me over, without the crap about wanting to see me, which although it may have been partly true, we both knew was only part of the story; and that was when he told me this story, which, if I had seen it in a movie, I would have said was too far fetched. I knew little of DNA, and less of the mysteries of twins, but I did know my friend, and I knew that if he believed something strange was occurring, then it was; so after listening to a brief outline of the tale, I told him to forget the whole thing for tonight and just concentrate on his cards, otherwise he'd lose more than usual; which of course started a whole new argument about who was the better card player, which although we both knew was me, was our ongoing ritual, the verbal part of which Doc would win, as always, with his powers of speech and deduction, but the practical was only ever going to go one way, and we both knew that; that's why tonight we'd sit at separate tables, that way when Doc lost, it wouldn't be me with his money, and when I won, it wouldn't be his money I'd be going home with. Doc would go pick up Elizabeth and I would meet them at the restaurant, giving me a little time to assimilate, or giving the two of them time to discuss me in private, maybe he was helping her dress, who knows?

As I showered and changed at his apartment, and dressed for the evening, I couldn't help but wonder at the tall tale he'd told me, and also as to my friends balance of mind; had he been dealing with the harsh side of life too long without a break, and it had finally thrown him, or was there something in what he was thinking; some kind of apparition or mysterious unknown twin of his new paramour, that was trotting all over greater L.A. and causing chaos in the police department; no surely not, but then you know me, I can't discount anything, and if Doc believed it, then there was always that possibility it was true, so I'd hang around long enough to see if his theory carried any weight, and if there was even that small possibility of chance, after all that was what I lived for wasn't it, the chance, and buying the ticket, whatever the prize. Before too much longer, I was to realise only too well, that chance, whenever it reared its head could bring all kinds of luck, good, bad, and bloody awful, but right then, I didn't know just what kind of chance we were both letting ourselves in for.

As we were celebrating Elizabeth's 18th birthday, Elizabeth was selecting the restaurant, this would give me some further insight into Zach's new obsession, her choice of dining establishment.

Elizabeth had chosen the Empress Pavilion, which suited me fine, I love Chinese and Zach and I had eaten there before, they do great Dim-Sum, and we could indulge ourselves now that we had something to celebrate.

I was there early, and just sampling a nice cold Montrachet when they arrived, as they walked across the restaurant towards our table, I could see straightaway what Zach saw in her, she wasn't just beautiful, she was truly stunning; but it wasn't just that, or even that, it was the eyes, aqua eyes, so unexpected and they took in the whole place including me, in that short walk, and they sparkled with life, they were worldly eyes, even at her age, and they spoke, they said, 'Come on world; show me what you've got, whatever it is, and I'll take it all in and give it right back'.

As I stood to great them, she came and hugged me and kissed my cheek, and despite her age, she smelt of woman, all perfume and life and assurance; as we sat down I caught Zach's eye and smiled my approval, and saw the relief flood his face, he'd relax now, and the evening would go well.

We spoke of simple things as we perused the menu and ordered, and then as we awaited the first course, the girl expressed an interest in my living, and asked me what it was like to play cards as a job; that took care of the time we waited for the food to be served, you know me, there's nothing I like better than talking about myself and the way I run my life; she was attentive and from her questions, intelligent, and retained information easily; Zach hardly got a word in, except when he explained how we had first met and become friends, and from the way she gazed at him attentively as he spoke; I guessed that it wasn't all one way traffic, this love thing, she thought a lot of him too, and I knew right then that anything I had to say about the dangers of their relationship would go right over both their heads, Oh well, such is life, that's why we buy the ticket I guess, if it were easy and simple, it would all be very boring.

We had some more good wine with the rest of our meal, and by the time we were on coffee, the girl came out with a simple request when Zach asked what she wanted to do for the rest of the evening; I think he had in mind dancing and bed, and may have been surprised by her answer.

"I'd like to go somewhere and watch Chance play cards," she'd said, which caught us both a little by surprise, and I saw him frown a little and look across to me, waiting for me to put her off; but it was then that I knew that at sometime this girl may just come between us in some way, because I found myself wanting to show off for her, wanting to take her with me, and let her see how good I was, after all, what man could resist a girl who actually wanted to watch him do what he was good at?

So, at a little after eleven, we found ourselves in a cab, heading for a club I knew, where you could play all kinds of games. Was it legal? Well no actually, not in L.A. but then we had a get out of jail card, or in fact two, It was used by a lot of rich and influential people, which gave it a kind of respectability, and meant the cops left it pretty much alone, and if by any chance they didn't, we had Zach with us, and they'd hardly take down one of their own, would they?

So, we found ourselves inside this rather plush Beverley Hills club, the owner of which was an old poker buddy of mine from his days in London, and we were made very welcome, and as word went around, several players were eager to make the sit down of ten grand at the table, and try their luck against this upstart Englishman at a game they considered very much their own; and so there we were, me at seat three, ten thousand dollars in chips in front of me, Zach and Elizabeth seated behind me as spectators, and my opening hand the Ace King of hearts, how much better could life get?

But then, there's always something isn't there, some unknown that creeps into the equation and just changes the odds, and unsettles your plans; little did I know as I began to play, and turned to smile at them, that as I gazed into the face of Elizabeth, that it would be her who would be the unknown additive, and her that would turn all of our worlds upside down, even without trying.

But that's it isn't it, and as we've already discovered, even if I had known, I'd still have bought the ticket, still have tried for the prize, that's the gamble, that's my life, that's the chance.

CHAPTER TWENTY
~Elizabeth~

18, what a strange number—Suddenly in the blink of an eye, I was 'legal'. I had had my driver's license for two years, but now I could vote, but not purchase alcohol, not in California—how strange our American society is. I could now have a relationship with Zach (or anyone else) without society raising an eyebrow or hauling anyone away. In Paris, I had been able to do as I pleased from the moment I stepped on French soil, already; the Europeans seemed to think I was old enough to make my own decisions. Now I had come to this glorious number—everything was finally slipping into place in my life, sort of like those sliding puzzles we play with in childhood, I could finally decipher the picture. My worries were behind me—well sort of. The parents were out of the picture as was the disgusting Lex Mungo. I still regretted having to practice on Shannon, but, it had been just one of the necessities of life. Shannon had faded from my mind as she had faded from the headlines. Zach had explained cold cases are still open cases and that he was still exploring the murders, he felt certain there was a common thread somewhere and he was worried for my safety. Oh, how I love him! And now, at last, I was going to meet the mysterious friend—Richard Chance. I was intrigued by the thought of someone who held such an important place in Zach's life, he never mentioned other friends, but Chance seemed to come up all the time—he had made some kind of mark, had branded my man's life with his presence, and I wanted to understand it. I wanted to understand Chance—it was a necessity.

I had found more new diary entries—mainly concerning Gail Hoyle—I wondered, was Lizzie upset that someone from HER home state was even talking about Fall River? Gail's constant flow of reminiscences didn't really bother me; in fact I was beginning to feel as though her family was MINE. Lizzie's thoughts of her former lover, the English pianist, had slowed down, but with the coming of Gail Hoyle and her constant mentions of Fall River, Lizzie's angry memories seem to be surfacing. I felt that she saw Gail as the stepmother she had so despised, and it was crowding the happy memories of her lover out—Had my love affair with my wonderful Zach sated her needs as on that point? I again wondered if Zach was a receiver too—had the spirit of Lizzie's lover possessed him as Lizzie's spirit had slid into me, and if it had—did he love ME or did the musician love Lizzie through me? It was getting too complicated in my head, in my body—I felt...CROWDED.

My birthday dinner—MY night, MY choice, and I of course chose the Empress Pavilion, the place Zach had taken me months ago, where we laughed about his rendition of CHOPSTCKS that had won my heart. I wondered how Chance would react to my choice; did they even have Dim Sum in

England? His being an Englishman also fascinated me—I knew Zach's mother was English and wanted to absorb the flavour of life 'across the pond' as Zach said when speaking of his birth place. He couldn't describe Chance physically; I don't believe that men think that way about other men—or maybe he just enjoyed keeping me guessing.

I knew Chance right off, description or not, I would have known him as a stand out. He was not overly noticeable, unless you were looking for him. Did he mean to be unobtrusive I wondered as we approached the restaurant, where we were greeted as family, which our frequent visits had made us. My eyes locked with Chance as the proprietor, Ken Poon, hugged both Zach and I. I saw him trying to read me as I was scrutinising him. Was this a part of his card playing prowess that Zach had told me about? I wanted to hear his voice, feel his timbre vibrate within in me—then I would know him—or begin to know.

I left Mr. Poon with Zach and went immediately to Chance, who rose from his seat at my approach. I ignored his outstretched hand, though I took notice of his beautiful hands, the pianist fingers which played their tune on cards as surely as Zach's did on the piano and on my body, I briefly wondered what melody Chance would play on me and kissed his cheek as I embraced him warmly. I had been told the English were rather cold, but after only a slight pause, Chance was returning my affectionate greeting, letting me melt into him, and when he spoke I melted completely – there was a magic in the precise English accent—just his "You would be Elizabeth." whispered in my ear, I couldn't tell if it was a statement or an accusation, but it won me over—the words seemed to wash over my soul and I could feel he accepted me and I accepted him as a part of my life too, I didn't then realize what an important role he would play.

When Zach asked me what I wanted to do after dinner, I decided to push the envelope a bit and said I wanted to see Chance play cards, and it was true, I wanted to watch him put on the poker face I had heard about, something that was impossible for my darling Zach—I was sure other players could see through him like I could. But Chance, I could feel that Chance could hide things as well as I could, I thought perhaps he was someone I could trust with my secrets—but I needed to see him in action, displaying his abilities on the playing field in a manner of thinking.

I felt my own persona change, adjust to my surroundings as we entered the card venue. It reeked of money, of the hunger for money, although everyone thought they were covering their stench—only Chance really was—I got the feeling it really wasn't a life or death thing with him and that made him feel very powerful to me, and I suspect to the entire room. It was intoxicating just sitting behind Chance, feeling the animosity his reputation carried as he bought into the game. I was being an uninterested onlooker, a sort of talisman for Chance as I believed him into getting a strong, winning hand. I felt his competitors glancing curiously at me and at Zach—it felt almost as if I was his date and Zach a bodyguard. Once again I was in an old black and white film as I posed nonchalantly for the onlookers, a piece of eye candy to distract other players as I brought magic to Chance's amazing fingers, and he brought magic to me, just watching him was being in the presence of a formidable man, if only for a hour or two, Chance commanded all around him without any effort but the shuffling and drawing of the cards. Watching Chance play cards and the aura surrounding him—the seemingly effortless concentration was like the way I felt when Zach made love to me—he was one with the game, and the game was his to own and do with as he pleased.

Chance won, hand after hand, taking his occasional loss in

stride—it was all part of his game of life, and he seemed to win back everything he lost—only doubled, all without batting an eye, not a twitch, just an occasional drink refill and a nod to be certain I was still with him, a movement that was only for me. I studied Chance, his movements, those playing cards with him. For that moment in time it was just Chance and me, sharing some kind of great secret that neither of us would ever divulge. When he felt the game was dried up for him—the energy spent, he stood gracefully and thanked his opponents graciously for the game and collected his winnings. He then, still without so much as a twitch, strolled over to me, kissed my hand and handed me his winnings with a quiet "Happy Birthday Elizabeth." I remained calm, following his lead, until we were outside where I burst out laughing and hugged Chance and Zach together.

"You are truly amazing!" I gasped when we were back in the limo and heading back to Zach's. The words I had kept under control came flooding out, "Not a move, not a hint! And everyone was sweating up a storm every time you drew a card, played a hand! That cowboy was shaking in his boots!" I said, referring to a Texas good 'ol boy who had looked at me as often as he tried to read Chance. I couldn't stop talking, I was so wound up. Zach laughed at my excitement.

"I told you he was amazing! Taught me everything I know," He kidded.

Chance gave him a grin and commented, "You just weren't paying the strict attention your lady was. You brought me luck tonight Elizabeth." Chance was gracious enough to compliment me, but I knew better.

"You don't need luck sir; you are the king of the game!" I returned the compliment and closed it with a kiss to his cheek.

Zach smiled as Chance had the courtesy to finally blush after restraining his emotions all night, commenting. "You have made a conquest, my darling. I have never seen my friend Chance blush before."

"Is that true?" I asked them both, no response from Chance told me it was and I said quietly, "I will take your secret to my grave" and patted his wonderful hands, clasped nonchalantly on his knee, those sexy fingers burning their way into my heart.

Chance gave me a wink, something I don't think he handed out freely, and replied,"I'll hold you to that."

CHAPTER TWENTY-ONE
~Gail~

I tidied up in Elizabeth's apartment while she went out for her birthday festivities with Lt. Murdock and his charming friend from England. I hadn't met Mr. Chance yet, only spoken to him briefly on the telephone, but I found him quite the gentleman. I hoped I would meet him in person—Lt. Murdock had mentioned to me that he was a professional card player, Lt. Murdock, (Doc when we played cards) knew about my love of poker, we had played a few hands during particularly slow nights at the station—I always beat him, he did NOT have the poker face down like I did.

I was wandering around picking up this and that in Elizabeth's bedroom, she must have changed her outfit ten times before deciding on a slinky gold number that I thought was much to revealing, but who am I to say? I was hanging the various scattered garments when I spotted it. I'm sure it wasn't hidden, it was not meant to be a private thing, it was on her bed under the pile of discarded gowns — it was just an old, leather bound book and I am a bit of an antique lover so I reached for it. My hand had almost reached it when I felt the sudden icy chill. I'm not the least bit superstitious — spent too many years convincing my children and grandchildren there are no such thing as ghosts to believe in them myself. But this chill, the sudden icy wind that suddenly blew through me was NOT connected to air conditioners; it was something I had never felt before. I moved my hand away from the book to hug myself and it stopped as suddenly as it had appeared…I reached for the book again, there was the icy breeze. I must admit it was a little spooky! I left the bedroom.

I decided to tackle the small kitchen, bake one of my famous pies — I had purchased some fresh raspberries and strawberries at the farmers market this morning, it would keep me occupied and my mind off of sudden cold breezes from nowhere. I chuckled at myself and my foolish thoughts as I gathered what I would need from the pantry and refrigerator. Baking always made me feel better, it was something I did well and it was always appreciated, but this time, the usual joy of measuring, mixing, and creating something that would be a treat for someone just wasn't there. It was as if a mood of hopelessness had suddenly befallen my spirit — baking was a chore instead of a joyful distraction. I thought of my daughter and her two boys, so far away in Fall River and began to wonder why I had ever left, what had made me think California sunshine could replace a family that loved me. I didn't get to see Ellery and his children nearly as much as I wanted, his shrew of a wife made sure of that! As I picked up a knife to trim the edges of my pie crust a sense of anger entered my thoughts, I wanted to slice my daughter in law out of my son's life — I could help Ellery raise those children. I brushed that thought away — where had it come from? Then a hopelessness swept over me and I thought how much easier it would be to slice through my carotid artery, end this ridiculous game of living such an empty life, I was transfixed by the gleaming knife, held it to my neck to feel the cold sharpness, took a deep breath, held it and—

The phone rang and I dropped the knife that I had been staring at in a frighteningly serious way. I picked up the phone and heard Lt. Murdock's voice saying something about going to a card game. I tried to answer in a normal tone but if I could hear the way my voice was trembling, I was certain he could too.

"Gail? Is everything alright there?" He sounded very worried and it was a relief to hear another human voice, and one that sounded concerned for my safety.

"Yes, yes, everything is fine sir, just doing some baking then I think I'll be off to bed. You have a lovely time."

I hung up the phone and checked on my pie—done to a turn. I felt better just looking at my beautiful creation. I got the oven mitts and took out my treat, setting it on a wire cooling rack. I suddenly made up my mind. I would have another go at that leather bound book, without Elizabeth's permission of course, she probably had no idea that it was an antique—young people today didn't take notice of such things. I headed for her room; again there was that deathly cold chill in the room as I reached for the book. I soon realized it was an old diary—and this stopped me in my tracks—it purported to be the diary of Lizzie Andrew Borden! I was amazed as I read the entries, flipping through the old diary was like being back in grade school. Of course growing up in Fall River we all knew the story—who in the world didn't? But if this really was an authentic diary of Miss Bordens, it was worth a fortune! As I read further, flipping through and basically checking dates, I noticed that there seemed to be some new entries, the ink looked fresh and the entries screamed out words. —The writer was obviously angry. Was Elizabeth writing in this old book? If she was, there went the value of the book, but then, all of a sudden, I saw my own name scratched on the last page—

GAIL HOYLE DOES NOT BELONG HERE! I quickly closed the book with trembling hands. Did Elizabeth resent me for some reason? Who else could have written that? I quickly hustled into my room and locked the door, silly I suppose, but that angry line had frightened me. I was more than ready for a good nights sleep, although I no longer believed it would come easily or anytime soon. I snuggled into the previously cosy bed having changed into my favourite flannel gown—I couldn't help it—I loved the feel of a well worn flannel nightgown to sleep in, and right now I needed a bit of comfort. As I turned off the bedside lamp and began my sheep counting, I heard the far off sound of something hitting the ground and forced myself to click the lamp back on and to rise and do a quick inspection—I found it in the kitchen—my beautiful pie was upside down on the floor. How could that have happened? I distinctly remembered setting it away from the edge; I had learned the habit from years of children and grandchildren. I cleaned up the mess, disturbed and suddenly exhausted. Tears starting, I cleaned up the blood red splash of berries mixed with fragrant crust and the smashed glass pie plate—"I must really be exhausted," I thought, and at that moment, retirement was looking better and better.

CHAPTER TWENTY-TWO
~Zach~

The others would no doubt, all sleep in the next morning; I walked Ellie over to her place and went inside for a moment, expecting to see a tray of brownies, cookies or one of Gail's famous pies sitting out, perhaps with a slice removed. Gail could never resist her own baking—perhaps the reason for her wonderful motherly plump figure, she constantly complained about how difficult it was getting to find a uniform to fit, but we all adored her and her concoctions. I was a little disappointed not to see a pie or cake sitting out, and nothing in the fridge when I peeked in—I was sure Gail had said she was baking when I had phoned, but maybe I was mistaken, she had sounded a bit distracted.

I stole a long and satisfying kiss from my Ellie as I saw her safely to bed, leaving with regret, but we both needed to rest—it had been a wonderful and very full night, but I would still have to rise and head in to headquarters in a few hours, it was like leaving a part of myself behind to leave Ellie, but I would see her tomorrow night and we would talk over the great birthday dinner.

CHAPTER TWENTY-THREE
~Elizabeth~

I fell onto my bed, it was almost the happiest I could remember being—only my first night with Zach outshone it. I felt the smile spreading across my face and my heart as I rolled over to check The Diary, which was now on my bedside table, I was certain I had left it on my bed. I knew there was trouble; I didn't even open it—it blew itself open to a new, very angry entry—I HATE HER—GET HER OUT OF HERE OR I WILL!

My smile evaporated and my heart pounded. This was a new infuriated Lizzie, not the great, great grandmother who praised my steps toward freedom. This wrathful creature was the woman who had murdered and was not afraid to do it again—through me. I like Gail—don't want her to be harmed. Gail was not a necessity, was she? I will need to go out of town in a couple of days, finishing work on an old film which was being finally completed, maybe I can convince Zach that I don't need a watchdog any longer and Gail can go home. I did not want another life to end by my hand, and I was not sure I could control Lizzie.

CHAPTER TWENTY-FOUR
~Chance~

A few days after Elizabeth's birthday, she had to go out of town for a shoot; it would only take a few days—it was a 'pick up piece' she explained and she needed to keep her mind occupied she said. Zach couldn't accompany her, Gail was expected at her son Ellery's for a birthday celebration and I had a big game planned for the second night, so we stayed behind and planned on a boy's night in.

As Zach was working, I was to take her across town to meet the rest of the film crew, so I called at her apartment around 8am to collect her, of course she wasn't quite ready, so I got to meet her guard dog, an almost retired police lady with a very interesting name, to me anyway, Gail Hoyle, and when I mentioned the Hoyle name being interesting, I was immediately subjected to twenty minutes of non stop explanation about how she was related by marriage to the guy who almost single handedly wrote the book on cards.

Despite the damage to my ears, she was actually very interesting, to me anyway, and by the time Elizabeth was ready, we had agreed that I would pop by sometime and we would play a hand or two, and discuss the merits of poker as a social exercise versus a way of life.

Elizabeth apologized for Gail's verbosity during the short car ride, but told me that she was a sweetie, which I didn't doubt, and we chatted about those nothing things as I threaded our way through the morning traffic, happy to breathe in her scent, and beginning to see how Zach could easily be falling for her, she was easy to be with, and hardly difficult on the eyes, as I dropped her off, she leaned across the car to kiss me goodbye and thank me, and I had that strange feeling again; I liked the girl, a lot, but I somehow knew, call it players instinct, that there was trouble coming, and I had a strange feeling that it was coming right around the corner at me.

Later that night, as Zach and I sat playing Gin, and indulging in a little sipping whisky, he began to lay some of the facts of the case out for me,
"This case is weird buddy, we have four killings, no clues worth a damn, and very little evidence of any kind, no DNA that we can tie in even if we catch someone, and only one connection, and that's Ellie," (Zach's pet name for the girl) "at first I thought, you know, that she must be involved but nothing tied her in except knowing the victims, and then when the last two were offed she was in Paris, so nothing there, there are ties between the victims, they all knew each other, and because of the child porn connections, I've even thought that it's maybe a parent of someone else used in their dirty little trade, but finding them isn't easy, these people are clever— disappear like cockroaches in the light of day once they pocket their cash." Doc continued, almost as if puzzling it out through me,

"I had shown Ellie some of the other films we found at the parents house, which upset her no end—having me see the filth she had been forced to wade through, but she couldn't name even one of the other girls they used, 'it wasn't exactly preschool fun time.' Ellie was in tears, so without ID, we can't trace the victims or their parents, this case is running up a blind alley fast, unless we get a real break soon, or unless someone else gets unlucky and the killer strikes again, and I can't face the thought that Ellie could be the next one up."

I tried to comfort my friend; "So, Elizabeth is the only tie in, and she was out of the country when the so called parents were killed, but maybe she is still the central theme here; all the people killed were connected to her, and in some way had done her some harm,"

Zach interrupted me—"Not the first victim—Shannon Toluene, from what I've learned she was as close to a friend as Ellie had."

"So, maybe it's someone who thinks they're protecting her, or wreaking revenge on her behalf, some kind of misguided guardian angel, she does have a way of getting under your skin…" I didn't know I said the last sentence aloud, but Zach caught it.

"You too, huh?" he was smiling now at the thought.

I slid away from that subject—Elizabeth had found her way into my thoughts, her scent haunted me, and it was all around in Zach' place. "Have you tried looking into her real family, any chance of tracing her birth mother, or even the father; maybe there IS a sibling somewhere, who knows more than she does about the situation, and why she was put up for adoption, in my experience, if people have skeletons in the cupboard, they're almost always old skeletons, things from the past that they've pushed out of their own minds, and don't even remember, because they don't want to, not until they come back to haunt them, and shatter their lives; sort of like sitting with Aces and Eights, you know it's the dead man's hand, you know you're going to lose, just like last time, but you play it anyway, because your mind won't let you remember how badly you lost last time, hell, even Hickock would play Aces and Eights again.

We sort of let things rest on the subject of Elizabeth and the murders and had a few laughs about the days in London and other places we had enjoyed in each others company, but I could see the Doc was still mentally on the case.

CHAPTER TWENTY-FIVE
~Zach~

Aces and Eights, I remember Chance telling me about the dead man's hand, the hand that Wild Bill Hickock had been sitting with when someone had shot him in the back, the hand disliked by poker players everywhere, it hardly ever won.

But, maybe he had a point, maybe we were concentrating too much on the now, and not enough on the 'then', maybe we did have to look back, to find the thread which connected Ellie to the murders, and maybe there was someone in the past who could help us at least. I had asked Chance for some new directions and he had opened a new door on the case. I'd have to go looking, it was the only way.

Chance broke back into my new thoughts, "So where does she come from mate, where was she born, that may very well be where the answers lie, and even though you may not like them all, you're going to have to go look, or this thing will always be between you."

"You're right of course, I've known that all along I guess, just didn't want to find anymore filth attached to her; I know it's not her fault, and wasn't her choice, but this child porn thing has my stomach heaving, and I guess I'm a little afraid of what may come out, but yes, I'll have to go and look, she was born in Fall River, I believe, you know, where that famous old case happened, Lizzie Borden, the one they wrote that macabre kids song about."

CHAPTER TWENTY-SIX
~Chance~

I did know; "Lizzie Borden took an axe, and gave her mother forth whacks, and when she found what she had done, she gave her father forty one..." weird old rhyme, based on an actual case which had been dramatized a few times over the years; some people would find that a strange coincidence, but I'm a card player, I don't believe in coincidence, things happen because they're meant to happen, coincidence is just our pitiful way of explaining what we don't understand; maybe Fall River would hold the answers after all, either way, I knew my boy would have to check it out.

As we sat playing Gin and drinking, the evening slipped away, and so did the subject, he'd made his decision, and that was that, for now; then around eleven we heard the approaching sound of police sirens, the whoop, whoop and then the flashing lights, as they got nearer, "Damn," Zach said, "can't concentrate with that racket..." he went to the window and looked down.

"What have you done now Chance; they're coming here, to this building," he joked and of course had to go check things out.

Zach disappeared to find out what was happening, and I began to clear away the debris of the evening when he came back, looking more than a little peeved...

"It's Gail, someone got into Elizabeth's apartment and attacked her, she's hurt, but alive, on the way to hospital..."

I had liked Gail, and looked forward to meeting her again, but she was new to this, what would anyone have against her, or had they thought Elizabeth would be in the apartment, I look at Zach, the boy was obviously worried.

"Do you think whoever it was could have been the killer, could they have been after Elizabeth, how did they break in...?"

He looked at me with a strange expression on his face, almost as if he knew the real answers...

"I don't know, but there's something wrong here, whoever it was didn't break in, Gail swears she let no-one in, and there's no sign of forced entry, so they must have been there already, and she saw no one; there's only one good thing, as she was grabbed from behind, she managed to scratch the perp's face before she went out, so there will be some sort of DNA under her fingernails, this may be just the breakthrough we need, all we need now is to catch the perp so we can run the tests..."

Sounds easy doesn't it and I guess Zach was right, it was a breakthrough, but somehow, in my mind, I saw otherwise, somehow I knew, things had just gotten a whole lot more complicated; we'd bought the ticket, the drum was spinning, and fate would pick out the winner; and then, God help them.

CHAPTER TWENTY-SEVEN
~Elizabeth~

Out on my own again, I adore Zach, he is the love of my life—but the freedom of not having to answer to anyone was so intoxicating—no one keeping me on a time clock or a curfew, I had loved the feeling when I was in Paris for those few short weeks that seemed like a lifetime ago. Now that I was 18—the magic number that declared I no longer needed an on set tutor. I was virtually free between my shots and when the set closed down for the day.

I hadn't mentioned to Zach or anyone outside of the film crew that the pick up scenes were to be shot in Massachusetts. The story of the film concerned a young woman (Me) who was haunted by an ancestor who had been persecuted and burned as a witch in Salem Massachusetts so long ago. I had felt a sort of kinship with the character as soon as my agent had given me the script to read a year ago—before the whole 'catastrophe' with the parents. We had just about finished shooting in L.A. when the Paris modeling opportunity reared up and I grabbed it, with a promise to come and finish up on location when called. I'm not too sure why I didn't mention it to Zach or Chance. I trusted them both, it was just some place I wanted to hold close and keep a secret—I felt that Lizzie would want me to go to her home if I could, and I should not tell any one that I was gong to explore that chapter of my past, as my character in the film was exploring hers. The exterior shots we needed were down and dirty, finished in 4 days.

I didn't tell Zach when we finished, I phoned him every night I was gone, speaking as if it was just another shoot, same old, same old, but when we wrapped, instead of partying with the cast I rented a car and headed for Fall River.

I suddenly knew the meaning of Déjà vu. I knew this sleepy town. I found a room at a local hotel, paid in cash, I had a portion of the money Chance had given me from his poker winnings on my birthday and I wanted to keep a low profile, I felt a little foolish trying to be incognito for no real reason but I didn't want a replay of my flight to Paris when they showed one of my films on the plane. A quick check of the local paper let me know I was safe on that count, and after unpacking I wandered around the town, being sure to go by THE LIZZIE BORDEN BED & BREAKFAST where I checked the hours for tours. They took place daily until 3 p.m. —I would check it out tomorrow...

Chance had said he didn't believe in coincidence. I think he has something there. I had decided to go into a small bar for a drink (unless they decided to check my i.d., but it was a hole in the wall sort of place, almost invisible, except for a decrepit neon flamingo proclaiming the establishment as THE ELECTRIC FLAMINGO and I took my chances.) As soon as I entered and glanced at the bar with its hippie throw back of a bartender, I knew I was safe—she had a wild mane of chocolate hair, with a few random streaks of silvery gray topping off a gypsy sort of 60's outfit, flower power to the max, and strangely she only looked about my age—a definite throw back. The décor matched the woman's persona—back to Woodstock sort of place. Very comforting somehow. As I ordered a Long Island Ice Tea the bartender smiled and just said, "You're walking home, right?"

"Absolutely, and I'm only having one."

She just smiled a beatific smile and murmured. "Groovy…" As she mixed my drink, a heavy set, bearded, fellow with long gray hair and a Grateful Dead tie dyed t-shirt wandered to the jukebox, where he inserted his quarters and called to the bartender.

"One for you baby." And the 5th Dimension began the melodious strains of GOOD MORNING STARSHINE. The bartender had a sort of dreamy sway in her walk as she wiped the already clean bar in time with the music and murmured, "Far out, Guthrie…" Guthrie put up two fingers in the international sign for Peace (unless you're Richard Nixon) and wandered into the pool room in back. I sipped my Long island Ice Tea and wondered if I had walked into a time warp. I noticed my friendly bartender had on several earrings, one of which matched the Unicorn necklace I was wearing. I don't quite know what prompted me, but I unclasped my chain and handed it to the bartender.

"It matches your earring." I said.

She looked at me, gave me that ageless Mona Lisa smile and just murmured, "You have a great power, very cool." And connected the clasp behind her neck so it could join the many others she wore. It made me feel—she made me feel, very welcome and I felt I needed to make the gesture. When she bent over the bar and repeated "Very groovy…" I realized that she wasn't my age—she was much older—the neck she had put the unicorn around gave her away. I was having a strange sort of feeling about this modern day flower child, and had to know more about her.

"Do you live here? I mean here in town, close by?" I knew I was stammering and wasn't sure why.

"You need a place to crash baby?"

"No, I was just wondering if you own the place or just work here or what?"

She smiled again and commented "I 'Or what', Guthrie owns it, I just hang."

I felt such a connection to this woman, I made a snap decision and said, "I guess I could use someplace to 'crash'."

"Cool..." answered the flower child, putting forth her ring encased hand, "Starshine—you can call me Star...or anything else you like..."

I looked over her gaudy, but glorious clothing, her explosion of chocolate curls and her amazing aqua eyes, and answered, "How about Mom?"

"Far out..."

I 'hung out' in the bar, observing the woman I was now addressing as Mom—the woman I suspected WAS Mom. Chance was right—there are no coincidences. I had a million questions for her as I watched her relaxed persona move about this contained little world of 60's memorabilia. The black light posters and multitude of attitude—an attitude of endless love and peace amid Bob Dylan, Peter, Paul & Mary interspersed with the Kingston Trio asking the never ending question—"Where have all the young girls gone?" It was NOT a long time passing here—it was NO time passing. Another long haired, 60's throwback wandered in with his guitar and set up shop on the makeshift stage across from the bar and proceeded to relive his youth through the words of Joan Baez and Simon and Garfunkel—the answers to everything were blowing in the wind and Guthrie wandered through—perhaps Mrs. Robinson's latest mark. He managed to pull me along into this strange parallel universe—a self contained anachronism with drinks and peanuts served up by a 60 year old flower child.

When closing time finally arrived (I had no idea what time it really was—time seemed to halt in this interstellar void) The guitar man played Bob Dylan's order that "everybody must get stoned" and Mom began cleaning up the bar while Guthrie started placing chairs upside down on table tops—an obvious signal that he was ready to have everyone GO HOME, which Guitar man emphasized with the Beach Boys Stoop John B. Too surreal, —but Far Out.

I followed Mom to her little shack about two doors down. It was a large loft with a huge downstairs and a top floor – it seemed to be made up of what was The Electric Flamingo's décor overflow—a fantastic collection of multi colored pillows, an abundance of which were paisley prints and Indian batik's. All doorways and windows were marked with endless strands of multi colored beads or ancient beer and TAB pop tops strung together. I wondered if Mom had simply hauled all of Haight Asbury here. The air had the familiar mix of incense and marijuana that was associated with the period Mom seemed to live in.

"Prescription use" she commented as she lit up a joint and popped an eight track tape of The Doors, Break On Through into a vintage 8 track tape player, and laughed when she added, "Guthrie is my physician. That all your stuff?" she inquired, nodding at my oversized shoulder hobo bag.

"For the moment," I answered, "I'm just passing through."

"Aren't we all? I never expected to be here this long."

"Be where? In Fall River, this flat, Massachusetts?"

"This plane of existence, guess I must still have unfinished business." Mom offered.

"Maybe I'm your unfinished business…" I whispered, "I'm Elizabeth."

Without even a blink she said, "What took you so long?"

"I had unfinished business too. I think I've finished it now."

"Groovy." That was all she said as she popped out the tape, unfinished and searched for another, maybe that's how she lived—just ending things when she tired of them. "You were supposed to be twins, you know, that's what they told me." She had put The Byrds—Turn, Turn, Turn into the 8 track player, maybe this was how she communicates, I thought., living through the music that had been her life, was still her life, "I named you Season," She said quietly, listening to the tape, "They changed it because it wasn't saleable..."

"They changed everything to make it sale worthy. They used me like a side of beef or maybe I was their trained dog..." I said quietly. Then the flood gates opened—everything about the way the parents had forced me to live, the unspeakable-spoken. I couldn't stop, everything came tumbling out. I don't know if I let it loose at last to make myself feel better or to make mother Star feel horrible. I told her everything—except about the killings that had been so necessary and Lizzie's Diary which had led me to her.

She didn't say anything then, just came and took me in her arms—the hug I had waited my whole life for. I stiffened at first in her urgent grasp, and then melted when she whispered in my ear, "I thought they would treat you better than I could Season, I'm so sorry it turned out to be a bummer. I still have the money they paid me when I handed you over. I was going to try to find you and give it to you, but you were doing so well financially, it seemed an empty gesture, you know? I went and saw you in films, saw how beautiful you turned out and thought I had done the right thing, that doctor explained chimeras to me and I sort of got it—knew you wouldn't find me through DNA and if you did manage to get to me it would be fate that led you, destiny is such a groovy thing, isn't it Season..." she was holding me, stroking my hair, her voice trailed off and I could hear the pain as she felt my pain, suddenly she wasn't my age—she was centuries older than me. I really didn't understand what she was saying about chimera's or whatever it was, but I knew she hadn't meant to hurt me—the parents had put on a good act and she bought into it—I couldn't fault her. I spent the night and the rest of the weekend with Star, fitting into her bizarre forty years past life style, getting to know Guthrie, his odd mix of clientele—his family he called them, and helping out in the bar, letting her dress me in her "Summer of Love" couture and braid my hair—those mother/daughter moments I had never experienced, except on film. She and Guthrie attempted to explain the chimera thing, how my DNA wouldn't match Star's even though she was my mother, wouldn't match much of anything as they understood things, which meant basically that I had never needed to be so careful in my planning, but hey-better safe than sorry, right?

I invited Star to tour the Lizzie Borden Bed & Breakfast with me, but she said there were 'bad vibrations' there and declined. The tour was more of my weekend of déjà vu –but of a different sort. As soon as I walked up the steps, Lizzie took me on a mental tour saying in my head "I'm your mother now, not her—this is our home" as I followed the same group of tourists reliving the chilling moments of the Bordens demise. I found myself correcting the tour guide or wandering away and breaking the 'please do not touch' rules as Lizzie guided me on a tour of her own. "This is where he broke my spirit" she said sadly in my mind as we came to Uncle John Morse's guestroom, then I felt her anger beginning to boil as the tour group entered the stepmothers room, "She knew about it—I know she did…" my thoughts screamed. And when we went back downstairs and passed a white dress purported to have been Lizzie's I said out loud, "It's NOT mine—it's Emma's!" The tour guide looked relieved at my departure. I headed back to Mom's and reported that indeed there were bad vibes in there.

I wondered with her what my alleged twin would have been like, asked if she would have kept us if we had both been born, and she philosophically answered "she IS with you—part of your Gemini being—logical that you would be a Gemini isn't it? Very groovy…you absorbed her, so you have her power in you."

When I asked about my birth father, she had a hard time answering, "I thought he loved me, he talked me out of following MY mother's lifestyle and that was a good choice for me—he was a stepping stone on my path, and he tumbled away when I figured out I was pregnant...I think his name was Ephram...At least that's what he called himself. Or maybe it was Bobby...I think he went and joined up with that Manson dude, I met him once—creeped me out—really bad vibes from that one, really a bad scene, got out of there fast..." she had drifted off into memory land, and I started trying to figure things mathematically—she wasn't quite old enough to have been an acquaintance of the infamous Manson family, was she? I began to think my mother was reliving HER mother's youth and turning it into her own, memory wise—or that she had tried one too many of Guthrie's hallucinogenic cocktails, he had offered me one, which I politely declined which drew the laid back proverbial comment, "that's cool baby". I never found out for sure who my birth father was and it didn't matter. As Guthrie had said one night—"everyone is on their own plane- we just intermingle occasionally..." Guthrie was the epitome of the love generation.

When I mentioned I should be heading out, of course the reply was "Cool baby" but mom took me aside and told me a story. It concerned the mythical Chimera, Hybrid Lion, Goat, & Serpent—a "very cool Greek creature" she said. "When you came out without your twin sister, I thought of that story, and figured out that you were a combination of many and would never be alone, you know? The lion is power, the goat is stability, and no one is gonna mess with the snake, ya know? They are all very groovy creatures and I knew you would be very groovy too. And a Gemini, it all fit and it's all very cool. Just follow where your other half leads and you'll be fine Season."

It made sense in a Starshine sort of way, and I'm sure everyone in Guthrie's bar understood it. Mom also gave me a hand painted t-shirt she and Guthrie had done in the usual rainbow of colors depicting their vision of a Chimera. "Very 'groovy'" I said as I put it on and kissed her good bye, heading out with my hobo bag to return to my rented vehicle and the year 2005. Did I have all the answers now? No, but I think Lizzie did…"it's time," I thought, "to take a chance."

CHAPTER TWENTY-EIGHT
~Zach~

    Sure, there was plenty to keep me busy; the case was enough to drive me nuts, what with the recent attack on Gail while she was in Ellie's place, then the powers that be breathing down my neck for some kind of break in the case, like I could pull an answer out of my ass or something. The damn media was having a heyday with things—the combination of my beautiful Ellie's axed parents, a 'sliced up to his pecker' porno king, and still no lead on the maniac who had left Shannon Toluene floating in a broth of chlorine and her own blood. All this in combination with the other loonies wreaking havoc as usual in beautiful L.A. had me working 24/7. For the first time in years, my abode was an empty shell without Ellie near—her scent was fading into a man mix which I was normally used to—but Ellie had over ridden it with her essence. Instead of the California cuisine of Spanish hacienda meets Barney Miller, I was out of sync with myself since Ellie had left town. She checked in every night from her film location, somewhere back east, but I still felt emptiness without at least a glimpse of her aqua eyes, the chance to breathe in her Anne Klein fragrance, a touch of her luscious lips on mine. God, I craved her like a lovesick teen. Chance tried his best to keep me occupied when I had an occasional moment at home, regaling me with tales of his latest win or loss at the tables he ruled over, but I think he could tell my heart wasn't in my laughter. I was spending all of my time searching for Elizabeth's birth mother thru the DNA sample she had given, when I should be concentrating on finding the killer involved in my murder cases.

CHAPTER TWENTY-NINE
~Chance~

When I heard what had happened to Gail and that she would be resting in hospital for a couple of days, I decided to visit, she had impressed me, somewhere beneath all the idle chatter was a shrewd brain and a kind heart and she had after all been guarding Elizabeth, had it been a coincidence break-in or had it something to do with this weird case Zach was involved in?

Stopping on the way, I bought two packs of cards and a small bottle of Glayva, which she had mentioned along with three thousand other facts, was her favourite tipple. Well why not, strictly medicinal of course. The American hospital staff didn't quite agree on it being of medicinal value, but somehow my "gentlemanly British charm" as the head nurse termed it, paved the way and Gail and I enjoyed the taste she had first experienced on her honeymoon trip to England.

She seemed pleased to see me, as well as the Glayva, laughing at how I had managed to walk right in to her hospital room with alcohol, and we settled into a rambling conversation about what it was like to be a professional card player, and the origins and rules of poker, well actually when I say conversation, she asked questions, I gave monosyllabic replies and she filled in all the gaps, that's what it was like talking to Gail.

It was however, interesting to discover that her husband, somewhere way back was related to THE Hoyle who was basically responsible for the original rules of poker and most of its etiquette, that his ancestry was the reason she had been to England on her honeymoon and she was very forthcoming on her enjoyment of social poker, and also the origins and history of the game, and surprisingly knowledgeable.

For an hour or so we played a little 'head to head' Texas Holdem, and she really was quite good, taking me for ten dollars, although in my defence it was somewhat difficult to concentrate with the circumstances and being bombarded with ninety mile an hour conversation, this lady would be a big hit back with the boys in London.

After a while she began to tell me about her life, and how she had lived most of it in Fall River, in the police force, and how its main claim to fame was the old historic case of the 'Lizzie Borden' affair, and how she was, "Amazed" to find a supposed Diary of the infamous Miss Borden in Elizabeth's apartment, had no idea that Elizabeth would be interested in such a terrible case, but you never know what will catch someone's fancy do you? Still she probably has no idea that it could be worth a pretty penny, well—WOULD have been if she hadn't written in it herself—well maybe it wasn't Elizabeth's writing, but it was certainly fresh...I didn't spend all this time on the police force not to recognize that! And I'm sure I saw the name Starshine Sunlight—I remember a woman of that name, it's not a name you forget—strange woman, she worked in an odd little bar called The Pink Flamingo or something, Hank liked the music they played, all 60's stuff..." and on and on she went.

As she spoke and I half listened, something in the back of my mind began to worry me, that whole thing after all had been about abuse, from Miss Borden's point of view she had been kept under her father's thumb all of her life, had an evil stepmother who had her eye on the money Miss Lizzie's birth mother had left her, and if the bits Gail had read in The Diary supposedly kept by Miss Borden herself were true—child molestation 1800's style, where children and adults made sure everything was swept safely under the carpet. Perhaps that's what we were looking at here; maybe Elizabeth's birth mother was still alive, and had discovered what had been happening to her child, or even her father, although we had no idea who that was, or perhaps she had siblings, who had tried to trace her, and, discovering what had happened to her, had sought some kind of revenge or justice, either way, this was something I wanted to discuss with Zach.

I caught up with him the following day, in a downtown diner, where we partook of a meatloaf lunch, and chatted over the possibilities, and like me, he began to see that somewhere along the line, it looked more and more like someone was wreaking revenge on Elizabeth's behalf; Gail had mentioned that the name Starshine Sunlight in the diary had rung a bell with her, she was certain she had heard it in Fall River—not an easy name to forget, so he resolved that a trip to Fall River was in order, to at least try and trace the whereabouts of her birth mother, and any other siblings, who may be able to shed some light on the whole affair.

CHAPTER THIRTY
~Elizabeth~

    I phoned Zach and let him know that I would be back the next day, he let me know that he had a new lead and would have to leave L.A. briefly to follow something up, but that Chance would be at his place and Gail should be out of the hospital by the time I got in. The conversation was a strange sort of he said/she said sort of thing interspersed with longing, each of us missing the other. I wondered if this was the reason Hollywood marriages break up so quickly—two separate lives trying but failing to connect up again after the initial whirlwind. I vowed to myself that this would not happen with Zach and me—once we both managed to connect on the same stretch again I would do whatever it took not to lose him. I didn't question him about this new lead—I didn't think there was anything I had missed, no stray threads hanging loose, so I didn't feel the need to butt into his worries. Chance would be there and I felt as though I had known him forever, I knew he could read Zach like a book, maybe, just maybe I would run with things—explain it all to Chance, find out what he thought Zach would think—if he would ever want to speak to me again, if he would follow his police training and send me on the path to justice (and maybe, perish the thought, a lethal injection.) I would ask Chance what he thought Zach would want me to do now.

CHAPTER THIRTY-ONE
~Zach~

After speaking to Ellie and finding out she would be back the next evening, I felt able to concentrate on my case again. Gail's ramblings to Chance were sticking in my mind, the bizarre name Starshine Sunburst, or Sunlight Starshine or whatever it was, seemed to beg for further checking, but whatever it was I was going to head for Fall River and check things out. I was getting antsy so I decided to fly out right away. I should be able to find this mystery woman and get whatever information she had and be back when Ellie returned. I thought. I hadn't really counted on the rambling mind of Ms. Starshine. Now Gail can ramble, but she still seems to make a sort of sense I can tap into.

When I located Starshine (yes, it's her legal name) she was tending the bar in a sparkling clean establishment that should have been encased in about 40 years worth of dust—talk about your blast from the past! Not only the décor, but the inhabitants of the place were vintage 1965—I know because my father had been one of those American Marines labeled 'baby killers' by their supportive homeland during the Vietnam war years. He was lucky enough to land the embassy appointment once he came home from his 1st tour of duty, where he met and married my mum. We lived in England until I was five, then dad was sent back to the states and of course mum and I followed. And the life of a military brat began. He seldom spoke of those years, but I knew he was bitter about what he viewed as his own country turning their backs on him and his 'brothers in arms'. Now, here I was, transported back through time to my father's worst nightmare—the return of the flower power love generation.

Now, I have always liked the music from that era, but this was a bit much. I reminded myself of what I was here for and overlooked the poorly, incense masked scent in the air. It wouldn't help me get information to call in the local constabulary for marijuana busts. I could take that up later, if need be. Right now, I just needed to know how this woman might fit into Ellie's life. Did she know Ellie's birth mother? I ambled up to the bar and asked if she was Starshine Sunlight? It made me feel rather like a surreal old time western sheriff that had accidentally walked onto Haight Asbury Street in 1965 San Francisco, Grand Funk Railroad was blaring out that they were AN AMERICAN BAND and all I could think was that this bar was an American dichotomy from 40 years past. To further the illusion the juke box suddenly stopped playing. The only thing missing was the nerve scraping sound of the record needle sliding painfully across the 33 1/3 disc, but my mind supplied it and I cringed inwardly.

The woman smiled vacantly, never really looking up and said, "Who wants to know?" Of course I wasn't in uniform or anything, but I was used to deference from the general public and this threw me a little. I'm not sure why I decided not to mention my detective status, but I somehow felt an officer of the law would not be an honored guest here.

"Zachary Murdock, I'm visiting from L.A. and a friend mentioned this great bar in Fall River when I mentioned that I was heading this way," I lied easily to the bartender.

"Who's your friend?" I thought quickly, deciding against Gail—she was probably known in town as a cop...Elizabeth? No, she probably would be an unknown entity...I took a stab, "Chance, Richard Chance—a friend from the U.K. He said the place was...how did he put it? Jolly good fun—a blast!" of course Chance had never said any such thing and I hoped he would forgive my putting words in his mouth, he knew well that sometimes one has to come up with the goods quickly.

The woman relaxed and asked me, eyes still cast downward, "what are you drinking?" as she placed a drink napkin on the bar in front of me and I thanked my lucky stars and Chance for coming to my rescue. I ordered 'the house special' without knowing exactly what it was—but it was advertised on a chalk board over the bar. As she prepared it I kept an eye on the ingredients (just in case) and then my heart skipped a beat when a huge fellow in a gigantic tie-dyed tee-shirt approached and slapped a meaty paw on my shoulder with a grin on his hairy face.

"Richard Chance? English guy? Does your friend possibly play poker?"

Well, maybe I had counted my chickens too soon. I put a smile on, swiveled toward the man and answered, "Plays poker a hell of lot better than I do—cost me a fortune last time I saw him!" I could say it convincingly—Chance always played better than I and usually cost everyone who played with him a pretty penny. The woman tending the bar let out a belly laugh that shook the whole building and magically the jukebox restarted with Credence Clearwater Revival's rendition of DOWN ON THE CORNER—was that thing programmed to react to certain statements?

For the first time the atmosphere relaxed, everyone was laughing uproariously at whatever had occurred. Whatever it had been, it had been taken well. Mr. Tie Dye was suddenly my best friend and sat beside me at the bar. "Man, that dude took me for two months worth of bar profits!" He said it with a good natured laugh, so I knew I wasn't in trouble for having mentioned a bad memory. He continued to the bartender, "You remember him, Star—Tall dude in the classy threads?"

"Yeah, I remember—I couldn't get paid for two months, lived off of tips—and he had left me a big enough tip to get me through it." Now she was smiling too, I guessed it was a good memory, obviously hadn't hurt too badly. I decided it was safe to join in the conversation,

"Yeah, that sure sounds like Chance—plays his cards with a steady hand, a clear head and follows up with an open heart."

"Yeah, very cool dude—reminded me of those street dudes in London with their card shuffling games," reminiscences of the eternal flower child. I was surprised that he had been to London, guess I assumed he had been born, bred and would die in this shrine dedicated to Woodstock.

As if reading my mind, the bartender looked up for the first time and spoke to me, "Guthrie here's been around the world in his lifetime, met all sorts and remembers them all, hard to believe someone can remember anything that happened in a cloud of LSD, isn't it?" I barely heard her—I was looking into her familiar aqua eyes—I had found Elizabeth's birth mother.

I chatted with the '60's crowd for awhile and when Guthrie, the world traveler wandered away I decide to take a chance. "I need to talk to you about Elizabeth" I said to the bartender, and saw her stiffen.

That psychic jukebox suddenly started playing Manfred Mann's BLINDED BY THE LIGHT– the calliope crashed to the ground and Starshine was blinded by the light of the song, clammed up—what the hell was it with the people in here and the musical atmosphere that seemed to rule them? I was getting a little pissed off now, watching her mentally rock out, absorbing the lyrics, and then I got an idea and wandered nonchalantly to the jukebox and eyed the selections. —Bingo! I selected SISTER GOLDEN HAIR, followed it with SPIRIT IN THE SKY and hoped I remembered the lyrics correctly; my mum had played them enough when I was a kid.

I wandered back to the bar just as my first selection began playing. Smiling at Starshine I commented "you know I did try to make it here earlier in the week, but I was so depressed I couldn't move—I'm in love with Elizabeth you see, and I'm afraid she's in some kind of trouble. I want to help her, but she has closed off a few parts of herself and I was thinking if I could find out a little bit about her past for her, well...maybe she'd let me in, ya know?" I had her attention, she was nodding in an affirmative manner, though not yet speaking—my second selection clicked into place—I could see her listening carefully to the lyrics and me at the same time, "Elizabeth is hurting inside—deep down inside. I don't think even she knows why, maybe you can help me help her—make up for any past mistakes before it's too late."

"It's never too late..." she said softly. I smiled kindly, she was responding as I had hoped she would.

"Well, then tell me a few things, please Starshine. Do you have any other children? Does Elizabeth have brothers or sisters?"

"Not entirely..." she answered, which was of no help whatsoever.

"What does that mean Starshine—Not entirely? Yes or no would help more." I kept my frustration in check; I didn't want to play guessing games right now.

"She has a sister—inside her..." another useless reply. Then her vacant eyes seemed to focus on me in a very direct way as my third song selection began—TIME OF THE SEASON. And I saw tears start to form in her eyes.

"You bring my baby here, I'll talk to you about it, but only with her here—I don't know you well enough to just tell it all without her saying its okay. She knows it all now; she has to say its fine for you to know too. If she loves you, trusts you, I can tell you about Season and her chimera..." with that her demeanor told me the conversation was at an end. Then the song changed once more—DUST IN THE WIND. What a fitting close to our bizarre meeting.

As I headed out I wondered what the hell that last comment had meant. What was a chimera? Some weird 60's symbol or something? As I passed Guthrie he gave me a 'high five' and commented, "Everything is dust in the wind man. All we are is dust in the wind..." I felt as though this interview was now worthless dust, blowing away in a warm breeze of marijuana scented wind. I hoped Ellie would be more forthcoming than her mother had been, it sounded as though she had more she could tell me.

CHAPTER THIRTY-TWO
~Chance~

He called me later in the day, after he had spoken to a somewhat surprised Elizabeth, who had returned that morning, minutes after Doc left. Elizabeth said that he must do whatever he thought right for the case, and he asked me to keep an eye on her while he was away, even though a fully recovered Gail was now out of hospital and back living in Elizabeth's apartment.

Keeping my promise to him, to look after both of them, I took them out to dinner the first night he was away, and after a good steak and a couple of bottles of wine, we headed back to the apartment, where a talked out Gail retired to Elizabeth's apartment and her own bed, and Elizabeth and I settled in for a nightcap.

That evening, that fateful, terrible evening, after Gail had retired to her room, I was actually about to go, and even now

I'm not sure why I didn't, because I knew if I stayed, I'd regret it, one way or another; but, something kept me there, a sense perhaps that she wanted to talk, to unburden herself, I imagined at first, of her terrible upbringing; little did I know what the real reason would turn out to be.

The conversation was a little stilted at first, we even touched on the weather, a sure sign between people who are close, that there is something difficult to be said, and that may change the relationship for good.

Imagining that she wanted to broach her childhood, I thought it might ease the way if she knew she wasn't alone, so I told her of my own early upbringing, the distance of my mother, the beatings, often with a strap, the being forced to 'finish' what was put in front of me, an overhang of not wanting to 'waste' from the war years, which whilst I understood, was rather overdone, being made to sit in front of a plate of cold and congealing green beans for five hours, being beaten with a strap every hour across my bare bottom until I screamed, and then finally choking them down, and being beaten again for vomiting them right back onto the table, and then having to stay off of school for two weeks while the weal's and cuts healed;

But that was nothing in comparison to what she had been put through in her manufactured childhood, as she began to tell me.

Her eyes had filled with tears and her hand held mine, "Chance, how awful…but you seem to be able to speak of it as if it doesn't matter now…I was beaten too, at first it was just what one might call 'normal' punishment, the odd spanking, and then it got to be more formal; He would punish me, while she just watched, unless I struggled, and then she would hold me, while he dealt with me, and all of course, as they told me, 'for my own good...' and then it began to take on the other form, much more sexual, he would excuse himself by saying He was teaching me, and egged on by her, would gradually introduce me to all forms of sex, usually straight after the so called punishments, when I was almost glad to do anything, as long as the pain stopped; but of course it was only a temporary relief, as other forms of pain began.

They taught me just about everything I guess, with her encouraging him to go further and further, and when he was spent, collapsing with that stupid, satisfied smirk, she would teach me, the ways of ladies, excusing herself by saying that she was showing me what not to do, and that I should always stick to His way of doing things, so that between them, they covered every kind of aberration known to humans, and then some that probably only they knew about.

After that, it was a sadistic progression, they would punish me in front of 'guests' saying that a little embarrassment along with a little pain would improve my behavior more, of course it was all just an excuse for their depravity, and their greed, although I didn't know it then, the watchers were all 'paying' guests, and not friends, as they were introduced.

Some of the 'guests' were then encouraged to become involved in my punishments, and allowed free reign to do with me as they wished, and in the end, I simply became the plaything of them, and all their so called friends, a mere 'doll' with whom they could play out all their fantasies, however sadistic and cruel, but by then, it had almost become an accepted way of life for me, I knew nothing else, I had been well 'groomed' and knew no different than acceptance. I had found my way to my white room, away from the depravity. I could go there and let them all do as they pleased—and I'm sure they did, it's all buried somewhere inside my white room.

I had almost not noticed that at sometime, somewhere along the way, they had started making home movies of my 'punishments' and had of course began to sell them to their friends and others introduced to them by the 'guests', until I had become quite popular within a very large underground circle. Stupid thing was I was getting legitimate film work too. Commercials, television spots, and feature films—and no one realized what was going on behind the closed doors, the drawn shades of that house. I was making loads of money for them legitimately and they were still using me to complete their sick fantasy world.

Then of course, Lex Mungo appeared, with all his staff and supposed technical know how and cameras, and all they saw was dollar signs, and a way of making more and more money from renting me out for his underground movies, assuring me in the process that it didn't matter what he asked of me, or what my fellow 'actors' and 'actresses' did to me, because one day, I would be a star, and they would be proud of me.

I was even given home schooling, in order that no nosy teachers would notice my introvert behavior, or the marks left upon my body by overenthusiastic 'actors'. Only Shannon, the tutor California law insisted on while I was filming legitimate movies, DID notice the difference in me when the parent's were away, I think she may have had an inkling that they were the cause of my silence unless I was 'on camera'. I opened up with Shannon—but never all the way, I had been instilled with the 'don't tell' mentality for so long I COULDN'T tell no matter how much I wanted to—I was afraid of the pain part of my 'family life.'

So that became my way of life, no real childhood, just making movies, which they could all profit from, and in between more lessons from the two of them, and anyone they chose to invite to watch or participate in my 'upbringing.'

As she told me her tale, I got more and more angry, my own Mother had simply been an alcoholic, pill popping sadist, but at least had never sought to profit from my misery, and when she drifted off into oblivion, had been more than happy to leave me in the care of my old Grandma, for which I had been eternally grateful, and had enjoyed my childhood immensely.

My anger grew and grew as she gave me the full story, and by now, although someone had beaten me to it, I would quite happily have exterminated these people and all their 'friends' from the world; a world which allowed them to exist, and perpetuate their evil on children whom it never would learn to protect.

When she finally dropped the last bombshell, I was almost expecting it, and in a way, it came as a relief to both of us; her, because I think she really needed to tell someone, and me, because I had begun to suspect something of the sort, and had some mad cavalier idea that now it would all be okay, and that Zach and I could 'fix' it, and that we would all go on to live happily ever after, but of course that only exists in fairytales, not nightmares.

"It was me Chance, I'm the killer, I murdered them all, it's me that Zach is looking for in Fall River, and he'll find out, and he'll hate me, and I couldn't stand that, I love him, he is the first person who has ever cared for me in any way, and I have betrayed him, and I don't know what to do..."

Even then, in the back of my mind, I knew it would all go pear shaped, and that what I wanted to happen never could, but I still managed to make the mistake of reassuring her, telling her that if she told Zach the truth, it would all be okay, and that Zach and I would help her, we'd find a way out of this mess, and find a way that they could have a life together, if only I'd had the sense to apply my card logic to the situation, it may have turned out better; but what would better have been?, them sailing off into the sunset, fat chance; Elizabeth turning herself in, and going to jail, and Zach and I continuing our friendship as if nothing had happened; about as likely as drawing a royal flush on the river card; but I'd bought the ticket, and I had to see what the prize would be didn't I, it was my way of life, and whatever happened, I couldn't turn against it now.

So I told her I would help, and by the time I left, and her tears had come to a stopping place, I had convinced her, and myself, that everything would be alright, if she would only tell Zach the complete truth, and that he and I would make it right. I should have listened to my old Grandma really, and another of her favorite sayings, 'Done's done, so why be sorry, you can't change it'...

When I left Elizabeth that night, she was calmer, and had promised that when Zach got back tomorrow, she would tell him everything, and rely on him to 'work it out', I still can't believe myself, a seasoned professional card player, I'd seen most things in my life, and I still believed in fairytales, I should have stuck to cynicism, it's safe; but that's the problem, the gambler in me always believed there's a chance, and while there is, we have to take it, don't we...?

CHAPTER THIRTY-THREE
~Gail~

I had been home from hospital for a little while, Elizabeth was off filming something or other, I couldn't keep track of all this movie making business, and Chance was coming over to see me, and play a few hands of cards again, I liked this laconic Englishman, his attitude to life and the way he never bad mouthed anyone, made knowing him and liking him quite easy, and when he arrived, we settled in easily to some hands of poker, which he obviously knew well, and had mastered as his way of earning a living, not something you could do, in my opinion unless you were good at it, the cards are very unforgiving.

As we played, and he easily won back the ten dollars I had taken from him in hospital, I sipped a glass of the Glayva he had bought me, and he sat with a glass of Hine, his favorite Cognac, although he had very emphatically told me that he never drank when he played seriously, as it could do nothing but dull the senses and impair his judgment, this man took his cards really seriously, more so than he did life itself I think., this also encouraged me into knowing this really was just a 'friendly' game—he definitely was NOT here to wipe out my social security savings!

After an hour or so of trying to read his face at poker, I finally realized that it wasn't going to be possible, but I hoped that I had read him correctly as a person, because what I was about to tell him, I thought he might not like or appreciate too much; I began by trying to feel him out...
"Mr. Chance, how do you see me as a person, more than that as an officer, would you trust me if you had a problem...?"

"Well Gail," he said as he continued to shuffle the cards, as a way of keeping his hands busy while he shuffled his thoughts, "both my old Grandma, and my basic instincts have always taught me never to trust coppers, but for people, it's a different thing, for individuals I rely on my gut instinct, that's why Doc and I got on so well so fast, we just knew we'd have enough in common to become friends, and trust each other, and as far as you're concerned, I wouldn't be sitting here, if I didn't think you were an okay person, and also a friend to Doc" I completed my shuffling, straightened the deck and slapped it firmly down with a smile and looked her straight in the eye, "and as I've already told you, it's never Mr. Chance, just Chance."

"Thank you for that, *Chance*," she smiled back at me, "and I think you know that I trust you, and that I feel you're a very good friend to Lt. Murdock; you know that most of us in the precinct think he'll make Captain soon, and he'll be a good one, we even think he'll become Chief of Detectives one day, he has a good mind, and he's very intuitive, so we know he'll do well, but something is bothering me, and I can't tell him about it, because I know how he feels about Elizabeth, and whether I were right or wrong, he would take her side, and he and I might lose the great working relationship we have."

I felt the hairs on the back of my neck start to rise, and a cold hand clutched at the pit of my stomach, I almost knew what she was going to say, I had started to have my own misgivings, and whilst I never have believed in coincidences, some things can only be explained that way, so I smiled at her and said…

"Go ahead Gail, tell me what's bothering you, if I think it's crazy I'll tell you, and it won't ever go any further, if I think there's something in it, I'll tell Zach myself, and you needn't worry."

She looked relieved at what I had said, took another sip of her Glayva and began to speak, hesitantly at first…

"Don't get me wrong, I like Elizabeth, she is a sweet kid, but somehow I just don't think she is being completely truthful about all this, I think she knows more than she's letting on, and may even know who is carrying out these terrible killings; and I know this is going to sound crazy, but before I was attacked in the apartment, I found a diary, I didn't know what it was, and I wasn't being nosy honestly; well only a little anyway, but when I opened it, and began to read, I couldn't believe what I was seeing; to all intents and purposes, it read like the diary of Lizzie Borden, and it could well have been an original from the worn and faded look of most of the entries, but, there was something very strange about it, there were some new entries, really recent, and they were in a similar hand, but not exactly the same, they mentioned some of the people who had been killed, and even suggested that they needed to be got rid of; and the worst part is that I think I recognized the handwriting, from a note that was left in the apartment for me."

I looked at Gail for a while, and said as calmly as I could, "Let's just say I don't think you're crazy, there may well be something in what you're saying; so, whose handwriting do you think it was…"

There was a minutes hesitation as she struggled with herself, trying to decide I suppose whether she could trust me and also whether I, and in turn Zach, would think she was crazy, and maybe even doubting her own sanity, then she spoke one word, and it was, somehow, the word I knew she'd say.

"Elizabeth's…"

We sat looking at each other for a couple of minutes, both of us knowing I think, that what she had just said would have a profound effect on all of our lives, and that somehow, our happy little band would never be the same again; and, after letting what she had said, and what she thought she knew, sink in for a while, I spoke to her in the sincerest way I knew how.

"Gail, I believe you, and I also believe that you really do think that what you say is true, and I'm going to ask you a big favor; I want you to keep this to yourself for a day or so, and give me an opportunity to speak to Doc myself, he'll take this better coming from me than you, and even if he thinks it's rubbish, after a while, because it's me telling him, he'll start to think rationally, and work it out for himself, and then he'll investigate the diary, and then we'll all know exactly what's going on." I paused and gave her what I sincerely hoped was an honest nod and grin. "Will you do that for me?" She thought for a few moments, and I could see her struggling inwardly, took a deep breath, paused, released it and then she said…

"Chance, you know I like you, and I trust you, but this is serious, and I don't want Doc making any rash decisions because Elizabeth is involved, or not, so I'll tell you what I'll do, I'll let you tell him, because I certainly don't want the job, but, if he hasn't done anything about investigating the diary within forty eight hours, then I'll have to tell someone else, and both he, and Elizabeth will have to take their chances, I like him Chance, hell, I love the guy, he's almost like a son to me, but this is murder, and I won't stand by and watch a suspect get away with it, without even investigation…"

She paused, and then looked at me with tears in her eyes, "Is that okay Chance, can you get him to do the right thing, and do it in time, make it easy for all of us, and be what he is, a Police Officer, and don't make me take this upstairs, I don't want to Chance, honestly, I really do want to be wrong this time…"

I smiled at her, as confidently as I could, and as I walked to the door to go and find Zach, I left her with a piece of Chance reassurance.
"Don't worry Gail, he'll listen to me, I'll make him, and when he investigates this, it'll all work out, and one day soon we'll all laugh at this."
Only trouble was, it may have convinced Gail, but, it didn't convince me, I knew it had to be me who told Zach, and even I wasn't sure how he'd react, but I was sure of one thing, this ticket would buy no prizes for anyone, and the chances were that in the end all of us would lose; that's the thing about buying in blind, sometimes, taking a chance can come back to haunt you.

CHAPTER THIRTY-FOUR
~Elizabeth~

I rejoined the film crew heading back to L.A. to wrap up things. I felt so at peace with my birth mother, with myself. Star had realized her mistake and felt the regret I felt was her due—she really had meant to do right by me, even though it had turned out so badly. Now came the really tough part—I had to tell Zach. Everything. Chance had been right, and I was certain Zach and Chance could make everything alright. As I sat comfortably in my seat on the film crew's bus, I pulled The Diary from my bag; I wondered why I hadn't shared it with Star. In her cosmic awareness, she would probably have been able to appreciate it. I set The Diary in my lap and prepared to read. I was alone, towards the back of the bus, I knew I was being a bit anti social, but no one seemed to care—the filming was complete, we could rest easy.

Then it happened, The Diary flew open of its own accord—the thought flashed through my mind; "Lizzie is pissed off about something." Her words blasted off the pages, I was afraid everyone could hear them as I could, I heard them scream in my head; "YOU ARE SUCH A FOOLISH GIRL! DON'T EVEN CONSIDER TELLING ANYONE ELSE! I AM AMAZED YOU WERE SHORT-SIGHTED ENOUGH TO TELL THAT ENGLISHMAN. ARE YOU FORGETTING WHAT YOU'VE DONE? THESE PEOPLE ARE NOT YOUR FRIENDS—DO NOT TRUST ANYONE."

I slammed The Diary closed, sat back and took a shocked breath of air; Lizzie had just knocked the wind right out of me. Was she right? Had it been a mistake to tell Chance? Would he tell Zach? And if he did, would Zach turn me in to the authorities? He WAS a police detective—it was his life, what had made me think I could trust him? Did a weekend of bliss cancel out months of planning and execution? I was shaking, had I written my own arrest warrant? How could I even have thought of telling Zach the truth? How had Chance convinced me? I wrapped my arms around myself, trying to allay my shivering. Then it came to me—it was Gail! That bitch had convinced Chance to make me talk—she knew something.

The Diary flew open again and I read; "THEN DO SOMETHING ABOUT IT! GET RID OF HER."

CHAPTER THIRTY-FIVE
~Chance~

As I took the lift down to Doc's apartment, I had that old feeling again, the one you get before you even look at your hand, that the cards won't be kind, and that you'll have to bluff your way into or out of something if you even want to stay in the game.

He greeted me at the door with his usual smile and inquired as to where we were gonna go play; his smile faded a little when I said that I'd prefer to stay here and play quietly over a few drinks as I wanted to talk to him, but he covered his disappointment well; Doc still saw poker as a spectator game and a opportunity to win, or lose, and hadn't yet grasped the fact of it simply being about 'the buzz', the kill, beating the other guy.

But he set up a bottle and some glasses, a good Hine, but he insisted on putting ice in his, damn American habits; we played a few hands, jousting gently at first, and then I began to speak, trying to draw him out on what he knew about the murders, and where he was going next, in his mind.

Brooks & Dunn were just kicking into "Play Something Country" on K92FM in the background, Doc's concession to my tastes, he was about as country as concrete, unlike me, I was a city boy through and through, had been all my life, but somehow my musical tastes only really took in the Sixties and Country, must be the poker influence I guess, and I started to tell him how I saw things.

"Doc, how are you feeling about this investigation, are you getting anywhere?"

"Well buddy, it's weird, the clues won't fall into place yet, they're all there I think, all the pieces of the jigsaw, I think, but I just can't piece them into a clear picture yet, but it's coming, and one day soon, I'll put it into focus, and nail this killer to the wall."

I looked into his face, the face of my friend, and one of the few people in this world I actually liked, let alone loved, and I knew he really believed that not only would he do that, but that he would do it whatever the cost may be, even to himself.

"You ever think of what the cost of doing this kind of thing might be? To you I mean, what if the pressure of these cases, and being around these kinds of people starts to get to you, to change you "

He looked at me with that steady gaze of his and a small rueful smile.

"No Chance," he said, "you know me, I was born to do this,

and it's the one thing I'm really good at, I'll chase this perp down and close this case, because that's what I'm here for, just like you're here to play poker."

As I listened to him extolling the virtues of being what he was, and saw the look of self confidence on his face, I began to realize that tonight was a turning point in not only our friendship, but our lives; Doc was a fulfilled man nowadays, he'd found his niche, and although he would happily continue to concede that my life was fine for me, he couldn't live without this, the buzz that he got from doing what he did, and being damn good at it.

"But what if you came across a case that became personal, that involved someone you knew, could you turn away from evidence, and make a personal judgment, could you let a friend walk away from something you knew they were guilty of…?"

"I'm a law officer buddy, could I turn a blind eye, walk away from something if someone I knew had committed a crime? No, I don't think I could, it's all about what you believe in, what you see as fundamentally right, what you base your life on I guess; why old buddy, have you gone and got a parking ticket…?"

He smiled as he said it, but I knew he was sincere, and maybe he did think I'd gotten mixed up in something and was trying to seek his help.

"No Doc, despite what many people might think, I wasn't talking about me, as far as I know, I haven't broken the law, not lately anyway."

I smiled at him as I said it, and he relaxed, realizing that I wasn't looking for help that he couldn't and wouldn't give me.

We played on for a while, but somehow we were both distracted, I think we both realized that somewhere along the line, an era had come to it's ending, and that there wouldn't be too many more nights like tonight, and whilst we were both realists in our own way, the atmosphere was tinged with a little sadness for what had been, and somehow wouldn't be again.

As we cleaned things up a couple of hours later, me a few dollars richer, Doc a few more dollars down, we hugged goodnight, as was our usual habit, and headed to our respective sleeping quarters, but this time, somehow, it had a goodbye feel, K92FM was playing my all time favorite song, 'A Soft Place to Fall' by Alison Moorer, tonight it had a prophetic feel, like somehow we'd all be looking for that soft place soon, but what the hell, the cards had been dealt, and we'd all paid to play, now we just had to see which way they fell, who won, who lost, and who walked away with the prize, whatever that was.

CHAPTER THIRTY-SIX
~Elizabeth~

I decided to take a taxi back home instead of phoning Zach or Chance for a ride—I could afford it, and I needed time alone to think. Everything and everybody seemed to be crowding me out of my own life—it wasn't MY life any more—it was Zach's and Chance's, even Gail's and very much Lizzie's. I didn't even want to go back to my apartment; I would have Gail watching me like a hawk. I decided to go back to the parent's house—I guess it's my house now. I needed to walk through it—see if it was clear of the horrible memories. The yellow crime scene tape still adorned the front door, so I tiptoed to the back. It was also tape festooned, but I slipped underneath and opened the back door with my key. No alarms went off, not a single screeching, whooping whistle or bells clanging, maybe there was a silent alarm set up, but I was past caring. It was like walking through a model home and as I traveled room to room, I knew I wasn't in the market for this; never again would I be a captive of these walls. I was free—almost, I felt Lizzie licking at my senses with an unending litany; "NOT YET, NOT YET, YOU HAVE TIED TIES. CUT THEM LOOSE—ALL LOOSE…"

As I made a last turn through what had been my room, wondering if there was ANYTHING I wanted to keep, I knew—there was nothing I wanted to hold on to here, nothing in my old life mattered and I didn't have to hold on to anything—or anyone. I had to brush it all away—go my own way, forget about Elizabeth Ann Morse. I took a deep breath, saw the house in flames in my mind—I burned that part of my past, and had to remove the other pieces that might hold me here. I took nothing. I phoned for another taxi to meet me at the corner newsstand to take me to Zach's apartment—I was clear on what had to be done and felt Lizzie patting me on the back.

When I got out at the newsstand, I began to have second thoughts. I walked slowly to the apartment complex and first peeked in Zach's window. He and Chance were deep in some kind of discussion so I tiptoed up the stairs around back to my apartment and steeled myself for a round of Gail's interrogation. To my surprise, I unlocked the door and found my place empty. Gail wasn't in her room, the kitchen, then I noticed two things; the bathroom door was closed, the shower was running—Gail's absence explained, and the answering machine had a blinking red light. I tiptoed over and pressed the button after turning the volume way down and heart beginning to pound, heard Zach's voice; "Hey baby! Guess what? I found your birth mother! She's great—a little odd, but I know you'll love her. She wants to see us both together—I think she has something to tell us. Talk to you soon." Then the message announced "ONE MESSAGE, 7:30 A.M. SATURDAY, SEPTEMBER 12, END OF MESSAGE."

Yesterday, he had left it yesterday. And what had she told him? I began to panic. Oh my God—what did he know and what more would she say? I had to get out of here before Gail got out of the shower. I had to plan. I felt my house of lies crumbling around me, and then heard the shower turned off.

"YOUR BOX—YOUR SATIN BOX!" screamed Lizzie, and I dashed into my room to get my box of emergency funds, the balance of what Chance had given me on my birthday after jamming a chair under the bathroom door knob—just in time, I just needed more time. Damn! Gail had been in here 'cleaning'—everything was out of place—I tore through the dresser drawers, the desk drawers as the bathroom door rattled and Gail called out; "is someone there? Elizabeth? Detective Murdock, is that you?" The door continued to rattle, the chair wouldn't hold long—ah ha! There it was, on the bottom shelf of the bedside table! I grabbed it and a fresh pair of clothes and bolted out of the apartment as the chair gave way and I caught a flash of the door opening and Gail's startled face looking toward my room.

I didn't even stop to think. I was suddenly running strictly on instinct—the survival instinct. I could feel Lizzie in my head, arguing that I needed to go back and quiet Gail once and for all, but I could only think that Zach had spoken with Star—what had she told him? Was there something she hadn't told me? Now I was running, literally, back to the newsstand to call another taxi. I knew they kept records and it might be a mistake, but I HAD to get back to Fall River, had to know what my birth mother had said to Zach.

Everything was a blur—I roared into the airport, LAX was beginning to feel like a second home as I rushed to the first counter I came to and breathlessly demanded a flight to Fall River or there about—NOW! The young man at the counter calmly checked and told me there was a direct flight in 30 minutes to Boston on American Airlines. "Fine, fine..." I mumbled shoving cash at him, "If that's the soonest," I mumbled as he counted my cash.

"Gate 41—hurry and you can get through security, No bags?" he asked, "well, that will be quicker." He smiled an airline employee smile.

"Family emergency!" I yelled back as I headed for gate 41. I made it through the maddeningly slow (but I suppose thorough) security check and onto the plane just before the gate was closed and collapsed, panting into my seat.

CHAPTER THIRTY-SEVEN
~Zach~

The phone rang and I smiled and said to Chance, "That'll be Ellie," but instead I heard Gail screeching in my ear.

"Were you over here?"

I held the phone away and told Chance, "It's Gail."

"So, I heard." He smiled at my obvious statement. I put the phone back to my ear and spoke, trying to calm her. "I can't understand you when you're screeching in my head Gail. What seems to be wrong?"

"What's wrong is SOMEBODY was in here! I was in the shower, I got out and the door was blockaded! I yelled out for whoever it was to open the door, thought maybe IT WAS Elizabeth or you, but had to smash my way out, I heard somebody rifling through Elizabeth's room, but they were gone by the time I managed to get out!"

I looked at Chance; he was as puzzled as I, "We'll be right there Gail—get some clothes on!" I could tell she was alright when she answered in a shaky voice.

"You two don't want to see me in my naked glory?"

I smiled and answered, "Too much excitement is bad for my heart. We'll be right up."

By the time we got there Gail was dressed, though her hair was still wet and her nerves were defiantly on edge. "When is Elizabeth due back?" she almost demanded, "because who ever it was DID NOT break in! Either they had a key or it was one of Harry Potters pals and they 'vaporated' in!"

Gail was right, I checked the doors and there was no sign of the locks being jimmied, the windows were all secure and it did look as though someone had been in the place—but only in Elizabeth's room, it had been tossed as if someone were searching for something. I wasn't aware enough of what Ellie had among her belongings to tell what, if anything was missing. Chance busied himself calming Gail, getting her a glass of something labeled GLAYVA, and heating water in the teapot. I decided to go back to my apartment and search through what Ellie had left there, maybe I could sort of decipher some sort of code in what had been taken.

CHAPTER THIRTY-EIGHT
~Elizabeth~

I had to use some more of my emergency cash to rent a car at the airport near Fall River and drive to Star's, I silently thanked Shannon again for her assistance in helping me set up that personal account, I had about $7000.00 with me. I phoned the bar and asked her if I could spend the night, said I needed to talk to her. Of course her reply was. "Groovy, see you when I get off..." I also phoned Zach and found everything in a tizzy back in L.A. Gail had startled another intruder to my apartment, he told me. "GAIL, GAIL, GAIL!" I heard hammering in my head "SHOULD HAVE TAKEN CARE OF THAT WHEN YOU HAD THE CHANCE!" I told Zach the filming had taken longer than expected and that I would be home by day after tomorrow at the latest, adding another lie to my plate full of deceits. No time to worry about that now—I had to talk to Star, had to find out what she had told Zach before I spoke to him in person.

I drove to Star's loft, the quiet of the night; a soothing blanket for my soul, which was suddenly locked in that white room again. Bad things were happening around me, trying to happen to me, and I simply could not let the bad overtake me. I pulled in behind Star's place and entered. I knew she never locked up; she was much too trusting of humanity to lock her doors.

Then it came to me. It wasn't that Star was trusting humanity not to harm her—Star was tempting humanity—daring someone to do her harm. I felt it in a flash of brilliant knowledge. My birth mother had held me as a secret in her heart all of these years, and now that she had finally met me, made her peace with me, she was, in a way of her own, begging to die! That must be what she wanted to see Zach and I together for, Star hadn't told Zach anything that would endanger me, she wanted to plead with me to let her die, wanted the hand that she had let go of all those years ago, to now help her into a more peaceful existence. Then I felt Lizzie, ever encouraging Lizzie, patting me on the back again and whispering; "YES, YES, OF COURSE SHE DOES! LET HER COME HERE WITH ME, SHE'LL NEVER BE LONELY, NEVER REGRET MISTAKES MADE, HELP HER ELIZABETH, YOU CAN HELP HER"

The door opened and Starshine floated into the room, beaming at me. It was as if she knew that I had figured it out and was so glad I had. She immediately enveloped me in a hug and went to sort through her bottomless pile of 33 1/3 records. She selected one and put it on the ancient turntable, plopped down on one of the enormous paisley pillows and patted the space beside her on the pillow, indicating I was to join her. Dave Mason began singing ONLY YOU KNOW AND I KNOW and I did know. She had chosen this song specifically to let me know it was time. She kissed my cheek and with tears gleaming in her aqua eyes, those eyes that were MY eyes, Star rose, pulling me up with her and began to dance with me around the room. The lyrics told the story;

Only you know and I know
All the love that we've got to show
So don't refuse to believe it
By reading too many meanings

Then she began singing with it;

'Cause you know, that I mean what I say
So don't go and ever take me the wrong way
You know you can't go on getting your own way
'Cause if you do it's gonna get you some day

    She danced me over to my bag, dropped my hands and continued on her own, floating through the room, a vision of the past in her brightly colored gypsy garb. As she floated she mumbled something about, "a groovy thing, I forgot all about it, this cool Doctor woman came by a while back—she gave me her card, and it's…somewhere. She knows about Chimera's…" She was rambling away and I reached into my bag and pulled out my long, sharp knife as the band played on in their musical goodbye to Starshine Sunlight Morse, she came up to me again, gave me another kiss—her signal, her goodbye to a life of regrets and I lovingly slide the knife across her ageless throat and watched her mortal life spill onto the floor of the room in a scarlet steam. I thought I heard her whisper "thank you Season" and I know she was smiling at me at the end.

    I found the record jacket, it had the lyrics of ONLY YOU KNOW AND I KNOW written ON A PIECE OF PAPER INSIDE!—I knew Mom had written it for me, in case I didn't understand her simply playing the song—but of course I had. I lovingly placed the sheet with her handwritten lyrics on her body. I was fairly certain that she would be found soon, when she didn't show up at the bar, Guthrie would come to check on her.

    I cleaned up, myself and the room, just enough to wipe out any evidence of my having been here tonight. I took my leave with no backward glance at the room or at my birth mother. I had granted her last request and all was good here. I would be back in L.A. by this evening.

I returned to the airport, turned in the car and was back on another flight, heading back to L.A. to face Zach. I didn't have that sense of freedom and accomplishment that relieving my life of the parents and Lex Mungo had brought me. I felt more as I had when removing Shannon from the picture had become a necessity; sadly accepting that my life would go on without someone who had tried to befriend me.

Now, the question that plagued me was—How much does Zach really love me? And what is love? I think Zach loves more than just my body as a love machine, I think he enjoys my company, but is that all that love is? Enjoying someone's company? Zach made me feel SPECIAL. No one had ever made me feel the way he does, like I'm WORTH something, something beyond sex and making money. Zach makes me feel human. The way he looks at me tells me he cares about what happens to me, the way he touches my shoulder as we pass through a crowd, offers me his hand, without thinking about it, not trying to impress me, just being Zach. Chance was the same way-treating me like a person, not a commodity. I was just a job, another assignment to Gail, but to Zach and Chance, I was a living, breathing woman. Or I had been— what would Zach think of me when he learned that I was the killer he had been hunting for, the one he thought he was protecting me from?

I argued mentally with Lizzie the entire way back to Los Angeles-Lizzie insisting that Zach had certainly not stood to the side when my body was offered, me saying that I had offered myself more than willingly with Zach, it had been MY choice, Lizzie countering back—what would he have done if you hadn't? Just taken you, like the others did! With that remark I tried to close my mind to Lizzie, but it was very difficult to do so—Lizzie seemed to be growing more insistent every day.

The plane landed at LAX and I phoned Zach, thinking I would prefer to see him at the airport, in a crowd, than alone at his apartment right now, Lizzie had again planted seeds that were quick to sprout and I mentioned that he should pull Chance along for the ride.

An hour after the plane landed and I was wrapped in Zach's arms, the smile on his face and the enthusiasm of his hug and kiss reassuring me that he DID love me.
"YOU OR YOUR BODY?" I heard Lizzie whisper. I brushed it aside and turned to Chance who also welcomed me back with warmth, but also with an eye that seemed to read into my soul. I looked quickly away, fearful of what Chance might read in my eyes, the man had an uncanny way of 'just knowing' what was in my head.

I said nothing about my birth mother, I had to let Zach bring it up—supposedly I had never heard the phone message. He let it out when we were buckled safely into his car and on the way back to his place. (So I couldn't run? I thought to myself.) Zach held my hand and announced it; "Brace yourself Ellie—I think I found your birth mother—hell, I KNOW I did! She's a little odd; no—kooky is a better word, lives in 1967 I think, or there about." He was smiling, and I realized he was right, so he must have spoken to her. I knew I had made the correct decision in sending Starlight up to the heavens she belonged in. Zach continued on; "She wants to speak to us together, I'm sure she's as anxious to meet you as you are to meet her—you DO want to meet her, don't you? Maybe she can clear up some things for us, she insisted she had to have both of us there together—so I was thinking we'd fly over today or tonight and find out what she has to say…" he was running on almost as badly as Gail did. I felt Chance watching me as Zach went on, not giving me a chance to speak at all—he was really excited. Was this the detective side of him? Closing in on his quarry? I shuddered a little, he seemed a different person, driven almost—THIS, I thought, is the man who will be made chief of detectives, the man Gail looks up to so, the man determined to capture the killer at all costs.

Chance seemed to sense my nervousness and commented "Slow down there mate, she's only just come off of a plane and you want to drag her back on board. Perhaps a day of rest before starting out might be in order?"

I half turned in my seat and gave Chance a grateful smile. "Yes, I'm really bushed Zach, can we go tomorrow or the day after? Whatever it is has waited this long, it'll keep another day. And I need time to get used to the idea of my birth mother being in my life."

Zach gave my hand another squeeze and smiled, relaxing. "Of course it can wait a day Ellie, I'll make the reservations for Wednesday and we can see your mother and explore Fall River together."

I felt my body stiffen. "Fall River?" I whispered.

"Oh, didn't I tell you that? That's where she is, where she's been for years and years I guess. She was actually there when Gail was raising her family there. Isn't that a hoot? Probably knew Gail and her husband, it's a pretty small place. We'll have to ask her."

I felt myself falling into that white room again as Zach went on and on. "No one can hurt me here..." was the litany playing in my head as we got closer to Zach's apartment.

I don't think Zach noticed how quiet I had become; I was in and out of my white room as he bustled about, packing things for our little excursion. Somehow we decided to drive to Fall River, I think Zach felt that would give me more time to become comfortable with the idea of meeting my birth mother, although he said it would be nice to travel together for a couple of days. So the next morning we were on the road, traveling at a leisurely pace (but not too slowly—Zach had a job to do—which just made me tenser with every mile.

CHAPTER THIRTY-NINE
~Chance~

As I watched Zach and Elizabeth drive off like a fairy story prince and princess, I felt a slight stab in my chest. I was either jealous for some reason, or having a minor heart attack, and as I had been pronounced in perfect physical condition just prior to leaving London, I regretfully admitted to the former. Ridiculous as it was, I was jealous of my friends happiness. I was also worried about what would happen to his new found contentment when Elizabeth, his darling Ellie, admitted the truth to him. I knew Zach, his sense of honor and duty would be crashing headlong into the glory of having found his perfect woman, his perfect woman turning out to be the perfect criminal, and having to make the right decision would be the most difficult task he had undertaken in his roller coaster ride to the top of the LAPD detective squad. I was certain that Elizabeth understood the importance of telling Zach the truth, but had I pushed her into something I somehow hoped would put an end to this love story, would break her heart and send her running or perhaps even to prison?

Perhaps though, I was mistaken about Zach. Maybe, just maybe, this time he could step down from his regulation enforcing, no exceptions to the law pedestal and see the side of the story that I could see. Maybe Zach would take a chance.

CHAPTER FORTY
~Elizabeth~

The closer we got to Fall River, the quieter I became. I was certain that this would be the end of my relationship with Zach, my one and only shot at happiness. He wanted me to turn myself over to police authorities, I could feel it in the way he touched me, so gently, lovingly, as if it was the last time we would be together. I knew Star would have told him too much—I'd had no choice but to silence that voice that would have ruined everything I had accomplished. Now, if Zach found out, if I told him the truth—he would insist I turn myself in. I had to get out of this—it was a trap, I could feel my life closing up on me again. Prison—I had heard all the horror stories, Lizzie had led me down that path, shown me what happened to a young girl in prison—I would be right back on that carousel of abuse, this time at the hands of other inmates or guards. Oh, Zach could tell me he would be waiting for me, but for how long would he be willing to wait? Once I was out of sight, out of mind, would he be willing to forgo the enticements of others? Lizzie told me NO! Men were weak, others were weak—I had shown her how strong I could be, I had been so careful and then—a moment of weakness, accepting the words of a man I only knew through a momentary kindness—and thinking it was love. I was being stupid. The Diary was my savior—Lizzie was my only friend, my trusted guardian. Lizzie would show me the way.

Zach was talking to me and I didn't hear a word he said. It was dark outside the car windows. Could it be night already? Or had the world around me just turned as black as Lizzie's mood, my mood. I felt myself becoming one with Lizzie. "...Far, a far off place." I heard Zach say, "Well, are you ready to do this Ellie?"

"As ready as I'll ever be," I answered nervously. It was now or never. He pulled up and parked outside of The Electric Flamingo and I tried to look startled.

"This is where she works Ellie," he told me, his arm around my shoulder reassuring me we were in this together.

"Zach I—" I began to tell him, I tried to get it out, but he stopped at the CLOSED FOR FUNERAL sign on the door.

"What the hell?" he muttered and pounded on the door, policeman mode I guess, and shouted, "Lt. Murdock, LAPD!" I cringed and he told me to wait in the car that he would be right back and placing me safely inside he went around the back of the bar. He was gone for what felt like a lifetime, but was probably only 15 minutes or so. When he returned he looked like I felt—devastated. "It's your birth mother Ellie; she was murdered in her home sometime over the weekend. I'm so sorry baby."

As he took me in his strong arms, I felt the tears flooding. I cried for my birth mother, for Shannon, even for that vile Lex Mungo and the parents that had given me such a distorted view of life, such a useless start. I wept because I was in love with the man who would be my downfall. I was lamenting all of those 'what if's'—What if Starlight hadn't given me up? What if I had told Shannon what was happening at the parent's house, what if the parent's had been normal, loving, generous human beings instead of monsters? But you just can't erase the bad things from your life, can't make amends once the bodies are buried, the tracks are rubbed away. So now, what if I told Zach the truth and he couldn't put aside his badge?

I realized he was holding my left hand. How long had we been sitting here, with me making a wet sheet of his shirt, using his chest as my handkerchief, had he been holding it all night? I seemed to have lost track of time, and then he said something that shocked me into reality.

"Would you like to meet Guthrie? He owns the place, I think he was a good friend of your mothers, it might be nice to talk with him, maybe she told him about finding you, about what she wanted to tell you."

He was back to the detective persona, looking for clues. It was a part of his make up, he could not stop it. Without looking at him, I answered, "No, not tonight, I really can't face this right now Zach. Can we get a room and go in the morning?" He patted my hand reassuringly.

"Absolutely, say, I have an idea. What do you say we check out the Lizzie Borden Bed & Breakfast? It just might be fun, in a macabre sort of way."

My stomach lurched, my body stiffened. Was this some sort of sign? Did he know something and this was his cruel way of letting me know? Then I heard Lizzie's voice, calming my jangled nerves. "HE DOESN'T KNOW, HE DOESN'T KNOW. KEEP IT THAT WAY. TAKE CARE OF IT." I felt my body relax, a reprieve had been granted. I softly said, "Sure, why not? Might even be educational."

We got the last room available that night. Of all rooms it was Abigail's—Lizzie's wicked stepmother. Mrs. Pruett, the proprietor, taking note of my red eyes and after a quick word from Zach, agreed to give us a quick tour, watching me wonderingly when I nodded knowingly at comments or shaking my head at others. As it was past 'official' tour hours and the other rooms were occupied, we could only tour the 'non-bedrooms'. Mrs. Pruett invited us to enjoy some of her home made pear brandy before retiring and we agreed, I asked if it was pear brandy because Lizzie had been eating pears in the barn THAT morning, which just got me a strange look from Mrs. Pruett. After having a quick drink with Mrs. Pruett (who could talk the ear off of Gail—maybe it was a Fall River trait, I thought) we retired to our room. Zach seemed to believe I was past the shock of my birth mother's untimely death and teasingly asked if it made me nervous to sleep in the room of a murder victim and I smiled back, "not as long as I have a detective at the ready."

"Oh, I'm ready for anything." He smiled as he said it and I thought that he might not be as ready as he thought.

Zach and I made sweet, slow love. He gently reassured me that it was all going to be alright—we would speak with Guthrie in the morning, and he was here for me...it was first time magic lovemaking—that same enchanted feeling of finding your perfect someone, hadn't Gail mentioned it?

Everything was feeling fine, it was going to work out, and then he murmured into my ear, lovingly, "Don't worry Ellie, I'm going to find out who did this—and make sure they end up in prison" I caught my breath, flinched slightly and heard Lizzie whispered into my head "YOU MUST DO IT" while Zach murmured sweet music with his body, I knew it was also the final chapter to our love story, which made it all the sweeter. As we both lay in the spoon position, I reached under the mattress. I knew it would be there, knew Lizzie would have made sure of it, I pulled out the same long, sharp knife that had left it's mark on Shannon, Starlight and Lex Mungo and silently drew a line from his left ear to his right, sobbing silently as I apologized to him, telling him that I was the one he was searching for, but I couldn't go to prison, it would be the end of me. I kissed his head, his brow, along his beautiful spine before I rose from the bed and washed my hands of the blood of my lover. I couldn't look at his body; it wasn't my Zach, not anymore. I knew the DNA on the bed linens would not be Elizabeth Morse's, knew she was the magical chimera child, an unknown entity. Once I was gone, the mystery would go on—unsolved, unknown, defiantly unwanted.

"THE WARDROBE, QUICKLY," Lizzie hissed through my tears, "DOWN AT THE BOTTOM, PRESS HARD" she instructed. I followed her directions without thinking, without looking back, and sidled through the sudden space where the back of the wardrobe had been. Followed the rickety stairs down to the now empty kitchen, where the empty glasses we had had our pear brandy in were drying in the otherwise empty basin, out the door and into the pale light cast by the sliver of moon. I looked around me in wonder.

"Now what?" I asked the night sky, expecting Lizzie to give me further instructions. No answer, except the crickets chirping their mating song. I couldn't just stand here. Zach's body would be found and of course I would be wanted for questioning. If I got out of here now, I would have a good head start—but where was I going? I had closed and bolted all my doors, burned all of my bridges, and now Lizzie seemed to feel her work was done. Had she deserted me too? I began walking along the road, destination unknown, just away from Fall River. When the sun finally began its slow ascent, I reached my decision—I had to take one last chance—with Chance.

CHAPTER FORTY-ONE
~Chance~

The phone rang in the apartment, and as I went to answer it, this time somehow I knew this call was the portent of doom, it wasn't the usual plastic trill of American phones, this time it had a much deeper more sonorous tone, much more the sound of the Angelus bell, which of course in many ways it was, as if the bell itself knew that the world would never be the same again.

As I answered it, I could tell straight away that she had done something terrible, and this time, there would be no going back, no saving of the situation, for either of us.

"Chance, I couldn't help it I had to, he would have turned me in, he loved me, but, he was still a policeman, he might think he would wait for me, but I couldn't got to jail, not to prison Chance, he would have betrayed me, it was necessary Chance, it was necessary, I had to…"

I didn't ask her for any of the gory details, I didn't need to know, just tried to quiet her, and get her to listen to me.

"Elizabeth, it will be okay, I'll help you, but you must listen to me and do exactly as I say, okay?"

Between sobs, hiccoughs, and incoherent babble, she managed to tell me she would.

"Alright, listen to me carefully now, go to John Wayne Airport in Orange County, don't drive yourself, and don't take a cab, they can be traced too easily, get the bus, and when you get there, book into the Courtyard hotel for one night, go to your room, and stay there, take everything you need with you, just a few clothes, but all the money you have, everything, because you won't be coming back, ever, do you understand me Elizabeth?

"Yes, I understand, but what are you going to do, what can you do?"

"Don't worry, I'll be there tonight, and I'll help you, you'll be out of the country by tomorrow, but Elizabeth, you won't ever be able to return, you do know that don't you?"

"Yes, I know, and anyway, what would I have to come back to…?"

"And one more thing Elizabeth, don't take your passport with you, leave it in the apartment, and leave it where they can easily find it, it won't fool them for long, but it might just give us the little time we'll need, got that?"

"Yes, I understand, and Chance, thank you, he was your friend…"

"We'll talk about all that later, now get moving, and do nothing and see no-one when you're there, not even room service, I'll be along as soon as I can"

After she'd gone, I tried not to think about Zach, after all, he'd been my best friend, so was I betraying him in helping her, or would he have wanted me to, and did he know how I felt about her as well? Oh well, all that, and any recriminations would have to wait, I had things to do, and not much time to do them.

It's funny the sort of people you meet playing cards for high stakes, and yes, some of them are what the newspapers would call, 'the criminal element', but you know what, when you need help, sometimes they are much more willing to offer a hand than many others.

I called an old poker adversary in LA, Dave Schultz (no relation to Dutch) and was told that I could pick up a good Canadian passport, in the name of Ellie Seasons within three hours at his bar, for only two grand, and for an extra five hundred, it would have a valid US immigration stamp, dated ten days ago, I went for the latter.

Then I packed a few of my own clothes, not too many, took my own passport, and all the money I had gained while I'd been here, and went down to the apartment garages.

I had borrowed Zach's keys, and would use his bike, a vintage 1972 BSA which had belonged to his father, purchased when he was on embassy duty, now Doc's and showing his British heritage, for this part of the journey, and leave it somewhere to be found later; I had to get myself out of the country as well, and obviously I couldn't travel with Elizabeth, or rather Ellie Seasons; I had to know nothing, if I could get back to London, via Mexico and Ireland, which is what I had planned, then they wouldn't dream of extraditing me, I wasn't a suspect, I'd been with Gail when Zach was killed, and they wouldn't drag me back to question me about Ellie's escape, not unless they caught her, and then the game would really be up.

Leaving the bike outside Dave's bar, I went in to find him there, with the required passport all ready, stamp and all; we had a quick drink, because I didn't want to be rude to someone who was helping me, and I knew that if the police ever asked him, he wouldn't have seen me for months, but sadly, I did have to turn down his offer of an afternoon game of poker.

Then I rode the bike to within two blocks of the bus station and abandoned it in an alley, and took two busses on a circuitous route to John Wayne Airport, a pretty little place in

Orange County, where I knew I could charter a plane without too much trouble, and too many questions.

The plan was, to charter a plane to Canada, for Ellie, from there she would move on quickly to Europe, then across to North Africa, where it was easy to cross borders without records being kept, and then she could move on to her final destination, which I can't mention for obvious reasons, I had even told her not to tell me, that way, even if they caught up with me at some later date, I could genuinely say that I didn't know where she was; then I would make my own way to Mexico, by bus, so it couldn't be traced, they kept no records at emigration at the border, so unless I was unlucky, why would they even remember me crossing?

From there I could get a plane to Europe, fly to Dublin, drive to Belfast, and cross on the ferry into Liverpool, without showing my passport, therefore I could have been back in England for a while, even before Ellie escaped.

As I entered the hotel, and booked in, I managed to see Ellie's room number, which would save me calling reception, or even bribing someone, and I had just one last task to perform, before I collected her, and using the Cell phone Zach had leant me for my trip, I called Gail.

She was of course distraught, the news was out, and Elizabeth was wanted for questioning; she even asked me if I knew where she was, but as I said I was in Pasadena playing poker, she fell for it, and made me promise to come and see her tomorrow, which I did; I felt bad about lying to her, as I liked her, but what could I do, and she was after all, part of my escape plan, and so, having put into place that I would call her after the game, I went to Elizabeth's room and knocked; this time we were both taking a chance, on each other, and on fate, and the next few hours would show just how big a chance it was.

When I called Gail again, she had reverted to police mode, and she, and everyone else were looking for Ellie, she asked me straight out if I knew where she was, and of course I told her I didn't, but I did tell her I was in the bus station, having played an all night game, and would be back in a couple of hours, and would help with the search, although I also told her that I didn't think Ellie was responsible; to which she huffed and snorted that she must know something, and would only be cleared after DNA and forensic tests, and extended questioning; so I told her I'd see her soon, and after going to the apartment for a shower and change of clothes, I'd meet her at the Precinct, and do what I could, she rather pointedly asked me to stay in touch, and I promised her that I would.

After buying a ticket back to Los Angeles, I waited and then boarded the bus, sat in the back seat and called Gail again, told her I was on the bus, and would see her in a few hours.

It's a funny thing, and most people don't realize it, but you can be traced anywhere in the world almost, if you have a cell phone and use it, and I wanted Gail to be very reassured, so I didn't cut off the call, but left it connected, then I shoved the phone down the side of the seat and exited the bus.

As the Los Angeles bus pulled out and onto the freeway to go back to the city of Angels, the connected cell phone was still there in the seat, just in case Gail wanted to check that I was coming in by tracing my phone.

I watched the bus onto the freeway and out of sight, just before the bus I was now on turned in the opposite direction and started my slightly longer journey to Mexico, and as it rumbled along, I cast my mind back a short way to those final moments, that last goodbye between Ellie and I, when I had let her go, in more ways than one.

CHAPTER FORTY-TWO
~Gail~

Chance had told he was on a Greyhound bus, heading to L.A...I arrived, in uniform, in my squad car. I watched as the passengers disembarked, happy smiling families with children that reminded me of my grandchildren, shabby looking teen age wanderers, businessmen saving a few dollars by taking the bus, young, fresh faced girls seeking their fortune in the city of angels who would probably end up in the endless parade of prostitutes who had arrived with stars in their eyes. But there was no sign of a distinguished English gentleman in a smart suit of clothes. I don't think it surprised me. Chance was a smart one; he would have known I'd be here, badge shining in the noon day sun. How Gary Cooper of me. I smiled in spite of myself, and decided to do a check of the bus. I walked slowly down the aisle with the driver, asking him if he recalled an Englishman on the last trip.

"Funny you should ask officer. There was an English fellow, very pleasant gentleman—but he didn't ride the bus—he came in and looked around, sat for awhile in the back, 'just thinking' he said, I think he made a call on his cell phone, then thanked me and took his leave.

Now I thanked the driver and went to the seat he had indicated. Feeling around I found the cell phone. He knew I'd trace it, if he had been a terrorist instead of a poker player, he could have blown the whole busload to hell, he was that charming. I pocketed the cell phone and walked back to my squad car, smiling. Who could tell—it could lead me somewhere.

CHAPTER FORTY-THREE
~Chance~

As that rickety old bus coughed out more pollution into the Ozone layer, and took me towards Mexico, and eventually home, I replayed the last hand in my mind, just as I always did after a game, win or lose; and boy, was it ever lose, I had lost two people who were both close to me, one I had loved as a friend, and one I had just simply loved; although I had never told her so, somehow I just knew she knew.

I hadn't even had an opportunity to say goodbye to Doc, but at least Ellie and I had managed that, however briefly.

We had said our last farewell at John Wayne airport. As I watched her walk away, across the tarmac airstrip to the small waiting private jet I had managed to get a seat on for her, in the name on the false passport I had also procured, and watched as she climbed the four steps and ducked into the cabin, with only a half turn of her head and a small gesture from her left hand, raised slightly, bent at the elbow, an almost wave; I wondered as often before, whether I had done the right thing, but then, what is the right thing? In any given human situation, the right thing is usually the one which we most want to do, and more than anything else, the thing I wanted to do was to see her free and alive, even if it meant that I had to lose her.

As I waited for the plane to take off my thoughts naturally went to Zach, who, at first appearance, would seem to be the loser, but then, he knew the rules, and I had advised him not to play the game, not to gamble, cards or life; and he'd chosen to buy the ticket, as we all had; and now here we were, all with a result, and none of us happy with it.

Zach buddy, remember what I told you, it's not about winning or losing, it's about the buzz, but the buzz only comes with one or the other, and this time, despite what people might think, nobody won, and nobody lost, it was a split pot, and that is the worst kind, nobody wins, and therefore, by my definition, everybody loses. On paper of course, you lost the most—your life, but you know what, maybe, after all is said and done, you got off lightly, at least now you're at peace, and won't ever have to worry again; and yes, it looks like Elizabeth won, to the casual observer, but, think about it; okay she doesn't go to prison, or the chamber, but, she can never come back, and has to spend the rest of her life being careful, and looking over her shoulder, and some day, somewhere, she may even think about taking the risk again, and then chance will come into play, play the game enough, and the law of averages says, however good you are, one day you'll lose; she has to live with all that, or not live at all.

As for me, well, you could argue that I came out with what I wanted in the end, but that isn't true buddy, I lost twice, the best friend I ever had, and a woman I loved, and I did love her buddy, despite whatever you may say about lust or infatuation, it was love, or leastways as near as someone like me gets to it; so, even though I get to see her get away, and get to go back to my life in London, don't go thinking I haven't lost too, because I have, and right now, there's no buzz, just an emptiness, and it's far from the feeling I want, just nothing there, cold, and alone, and weary. I won't be at your funeral buddy, couldn't stand all that police uniformed razzamatazz, and when they fire those blanks into the air, it would feel kind of like they were aimed at me, or at least my conscience, and you know me and guilt buddy, I don't wear it well, but we'll see each other again, somewhere around the green baize table of this thing we call life, or maybe death, hell, at least now you know the answers to some questions, me I'll still be wondering, so in that way you beat me, you're ahead of the game, just like you always liked to be.

And one of these fine days, I'll be back across the pond, and I'll drive by, and put some of those silly damn cactus roses you like so much on that big marble stone that they'll put you under, and we'll chat, and it'll be like the old days, when we used to laugh at everybody and everything, and think we were invincible; guess we got that one wrong eh buddy? One bluff too many, we should have folded when we had the chance.

Ah, there's that word again, chance.

CHAPTER FORTY-FOUR
~Elizabeth~

We embraced—was it as resigned lovers parting, brother to sister, student to mentor (ah, but which would be which?) I knew Chance loved me, I just wasn't quite sure how, well, we'd never know now would we, and I, and Lizzie had to get the hell out of Dodge, so I boarded the plane without looking back.

As the aircraft prepared for lift off I stole a look out of my window and fancied that I saw Chance looking for me, standing by the chicken wire they laughingly call a perimeter at John Wayne airport, staring up at the departing plane, it could have been anyone of course, from that height, but I like to think that even in the short time we knew each other, I had gotten to know the man. It was Chance alright. Oh yes, I had a reason to do what I have done, even though the first time was almost just for practice, to see if I could actually do it, see for myself how I would react, and if what I had in mind was simply fantasy, or whether I could be whom I thought I was.

As for the rest of them, well...Lex was just a nasty little pervert, a smut monger, who deserved whatever death, had in store for him; but them, the PARENTS, they were special, they deserved something special, that only I and the diary could provide.

They had stolen my childhood, my innocence, had moulded me they thought, into not only a plaything for them and their so called friends, but into a money making machine, to keep them in the lifestyle they had always wanted.

No doubt I was like all children are, naughty sometimes, maybe I even deserved some of what happened to me, but, if those early beatings were really 'for my own good' why then, did they need to be filmed, and sold to people to watch, and why did they have to be in front of all those creepy people who had paid them large sums to watch my punishment and degradation, and even after that, what was the rest of it about, that wasn't punishment, and it certainly had nothing to do with love, or even sex, simply perversion and profit, so they deserved it all, didn't they?

But then why did the other thing have to happen, why did Zach have to come along?
Oh yes, perhaps it was to show me there was a way out, through love, through appreciation, but of course by then, it was too late, wasn't it?

It was fun, and really different, to have someone who actually cared about me, and whom I cared about, but it couldn't last, not for me, could it, because, I'll say again; in the end, what made my knight in shining armor a knight, also took him away from me; what I needed was a knight in tarnished armor, and then one came along, and knew me for what I was, a kindred spirit, broken but self repaired, and then it all got out of hand and complicated, because the two knights, those two wonderful people, were friends and I was the inevitable catalyst that would test and bend that friendship, I was the ticket they both bought, I was the prize, but the cost of the ticket ended up too much for both of them.

As for me, will I ever be truly repaired, in either body or spirit, can I take my chance and run with it, can I lift the prize and lead what you would call, a normal life, and what exactly is that anyway, a normal life, damned if I know, maybe one day I'll get to ask Lizzie, she's probably the only one who'll give me an honest answer.

I settled into my seat, pulled my carry on bag from beneath and rummaged through it for something to read. My hand recognized the well worn leather cover before my eyes even greeted the welcome sight. Chance had returned it, he trusted me. I opened the diary and saw he had inscribed it, I recognized his orderly penmanship, "How British" I thought and chuckled as I read the inscription.
"*Life is a game of chance Elizabeth—I can't keep you from playing, can you?*"
I closed the diary, a satisfied smile on my face as I noticed my attractive seat mate watching me with eyes the shade of a forest glen. He smiled back at me and commented, "You look like the cat that swallowed the canary."
"Do I?"
"I can almost see the feathers between your teeth," he teased.
"Perhaps I should check my mouth in the bathroom mirror."
"These facilities are so cramped, I would be delighted to share the use of my apartment when we land, and I have a great deal of room…" The invitation was obvious in its meaning, I rubbed my hand over the leather of the diary, my fingers tingling," It's up to you of course." The fellow smiled again.
I relaxed, sat back and smiled again, "Yes, it is, isn't it?" I replied, adding; "Life is such a game of chance, don't you think?"

Printed in the United States
48130LVS00004B/10-12